A Special
Kind of Love

Cedar River Daydreams

Other Books by Judy Baer

A Special Kind of Love

Judy Baer

BETHANY HOUSE PUBLISHERS
MINNEAPOLIS, MINNESOTA 55438

A Special Kind of Love
Judy Baer

Cover illustration by Andrea Jorgenson

Library of Congress Catalog Card Number 93–72040

ISBN 1–55661–367-9

Published by Bethany House Publishers
A Ministry of Bethany Fellowship, Inc.
11300 Hampshire Avenue South
Minneapolis, Minnesota 55438

Printed in the United States of America

For Barb Lilland—
You're great!

JUDY BAER received a B.A. in English and Education from Concordia College in Moorhead, Minnesota. She has had over thirty novels published and is a member of the National Romance Writers of America, the Society of Children's Book Writers, and the National Federation of Press Women.

Two of her novels, *Adrienne* and *Paige*, have been prizewinning bestsellers in the Bethany House SPRINGFLOWER SERIES (for girls 12–15). Both books have been awarded first place for juvenile fiction in the National Federation of Press Women's communications contest.

"Lord, you bless those who do what is right. You protect them like a soldier's shield."

Psalm 5:12

Chapter One

"Do you think she's home?" Binky McNaughton and Lexi Leighton walked up the sidewalk toward Jennifer Golden's house. Lexi stared at the closed and unrevealing windows. "I told her we were coming, but it looks dark, doesn't it?"

"Where would she be if she's not here. . . ." As Binky spoke, the front door of the house swung open and Jennifer peered out.

"There you are! Come in. I've been waiting for you." Jennifer glanced over her shoulder toward the street before closing the door behind the girls.

"What's going on?" Binky wondered. "You're acting weird."

Jennifer hurried to the curtained window and peeked outside. "I want to make sure my parents don't catch me if they come home early."

"What are you doing that's so awful?" Binky looked around the room. Other than a box of photographs in the middle of the floor, the house was neat and orderly.

Jennifer smoothed the curtain closed and walked over to the box of photos. She kicked at it with the toe of her shoe. "I found this box in the attic. It's full of pictures I've never seen before."

9

"What's so bad about the photographs?"

"My parents' thirtieth wedding anniversary is coming up soon."

"Wow! Thirty years! That's a long time!" Binky blurted.

"I know. That's why I want to do something really special," Jennifer explained. "I'm going to surprise my parents by making a scrapbook of photos, news-clippings, and mementoes of their thirty years together."

"Are you *sure* your parents have been married thirty years?" Binky stared at a photo she'd picked from the box. "They don't look that old."

"Mom and Dad are both fifty-seven years old. They were married when they were twenty-seven. That comes out to thirty years. They married and had their family late in life."

"I thought by the time you turned fifty-seven you were practically falling apart or something," Binky said. "They look really good—like they're in their forties."

"Mom says age is 'relative,'" Lexi commented. "When you're five, someone who is fifteen looks old. When you're fifteen, thirty looks old, but when you're thirty, forty doesn't seem old at all."

"Weird. It's hard to think of my parents ever being young. It seems they've been just parents forever." Binky dropped onto the sofa and flung herself backward across the soft cushion. "Imagine my mom being my age! I wonder if she liked the kind of things I like."

"Of course she did," Lexi said. "She must have liked clothes, music, and boys."

"Boys? No way!" Binky wrinkled her nose. "I can't imagine my mom liking guys!"

"She married your father, didn't she?"

"That's different. He's my dad."

"But your dad was a teenage boy once too."

"Ohhh . . . gross!" Binky shivered. "I don't want to think about it. They're my *parents*."

"I'm glad you came over." Jennifer ignored Binky's outburst. "I want this to be the most special gift I've ever given Mom and Dad. Want to help me?" Without waiting for their answer, she lifted some photos from the box and put them into Lexi's and Binky's laps. "Look through these. See if you can find any good pictures of my parents and me. You guys are great! This will help me get the job done faster."

"I think the photo album is a wonderful idea," Lexi commented, "but why all the secrecy? Won't your parents let you look through these photos if you just ask them?"

"I don't want them to know what I'm doing." A frown flickered across Jennifer's features. "My parents are kind of weird about the early days of their marriage. They never want to talk about it. They act as though their marriage started the day I was born."

Binky looked at her blankly. "What does that mean?"

"I don't know. It's just a feeling I have. If my parents talk about the 'olden days,' they mention when I was a baby and all the fun they had then. They don't discuss the years before that. It's as if that time wasn't as happy. I've tried asking questions, but they always change the subject."

"Maybe it's because you were such an exceptional baby that you completely changed their lives," Lexi suggested.

"Or . . . you were such a horrible baby that they

forgot about all the good years they had before you came along," Binky added.

"I wish you two would be quiet and start looking at the pictures." Jennifer gave them each a dirty look. "Hurry up. I want to put them away before my parents come back."

The room was silent as the girls thumbed through photos and newspaper clippings. Binky giggled when she found pictures of Jennifer as a baby. Holding her were Mr. and Mrs. Golden in the popular clothing style of their youth. "Oooo," Binky squealed, "your mom's beehive hair-do is a riot!"

"I can already see my mom when I give her this album," Jennifer said dreamily. "She'll get all teary-eyed and blow her nose until it's bright red. Dad will just keep clearing his throat and saying thank you." She grinned. "It's going to be great."

"Here are your parents' wedding pictures." Lexi held up a large white album.

"I'll need some of those." Jennifer moved to where Lexi was sitting.

"Look at your mom's hair." Lexi pointed to a photo of Mrs. Golden with blond hair that grazed her waist. "Isn't she beautiful?"

The three girls studied the pages of the wedding album. "Your mom is really pretty," Binky commented. "She didn't look very much like you when she was young though, did she?"

"Oh, thanks. Does that mean I'm not pretty?" Jennifer pretended to pout.

"That's not what I meant, and you know it. You're gorgeous. Except for your blond hair you look different from her, that's all."

Jennifer stared at the pictures in Binky's hands.

"I really do, don't I? I've never thought about it before."

Binky startled Lexi and Jennifer by sniffling.

"Binky, are you crying?"

Binky wiped a tear off her cheek with the back of her hand.

"Sorry. I just couldn't help it."

"What's wrong?"

"These wedding pictures make me sad, that's all. They remind me of Mike and Nancy. It is so awful that they've had to cancel their wedding."

Mike Winston was the brother of Lexi's boyfriend, Todd. Mike and Nancy Kelvin were engaged to be married, but Nancy had been recently diagnosed as having AIDS and their wedding plans had come to a halt. Now, instead of planning their wedding, Nancy's time was devoted to maintaining her strength and speaking to groups of young people about AIDS education.

"Nancy's doing all right," Lexi assured Binky. "She's very careful about her health. She's got a lot of faith in God. That's getting her through this bad time."

"She's a stronger person than I'll ever be," Jennifer commented.

"My brother Egg has been at Mike's garage with Todd." Binky's eyes turned misty again. "Egg says that if he were Mike, he'd just break down and bawl."

Lexi drummed her finger against the plastic page of the photo album. "The Winstons have cried a flood of tears over Nancy."

Binky snuffled again. "It's such a waste that someone as beautiful and sweet as Nancy has to die."

"Well, she's not dying yet," Lexi reminded Binky.

"In fact, if she heard you talking like this, she'd scold you. Nancy says keeping her spirits up is one of the most important parts of fighting this disease."

Jennifer stroked the page of the wedding album. "My parents were certainly a lot more fortunate than Mike and Nancy. When I think about it, I realize that thirty years of marriage is pretty special. I could have parents like Minda's or Matt's, who've been divorced."

Binky made a face. "If I could divorce my brother Egg, I'd probably do that."

"You would not, Binky. You're crazy about Egg."

"I'm not crazy about Egg. He *drives* me crazy—there's a difference."

"Look at this!" Lexi lifted a bundle of photos secured with a rubber band from the bottom of a shoe box. "Here are some pictures of your parents and a little baby."

"That's not just any baby, silly. That's *me!*"

"Well, it's you looking like a sausage with eyeballs." Binky grinned. "You look like a little potato dumpling or something, all squishy and round with no real shape. Look at this picture!"

"Let me see that!" Jennifer grabbed the picture. "I was a little chubby back then, that's all. Mother said that I was the most darling baby in the entire world and I believe her."

"You were probably the most darling baby *dumpling* in the whole world."

"If you can't say something nice, don't say anything at all."

"Okay. So maybe you weren't a dumpling. But you *did* resemble a sausage. . . ."

Lexi took the picture out of Binky's hand. "Let's

see what it says on the back." She flipped the picture over. In Mrs. Golden's handwriting were the words "the day Jennifer came to us."

"That must be the day I came home from the hospital."

"You were really a big baby, weren't you?"

Jennifer glared at Binky. "First you called me a dumpling, then a sausage; now you call me fat!"

"Touchy, touchy." Binky reached into the box and came up with another photo. "Look at this!" She held out a photo of a naked baby Jennifer posed on a bearskin rug. "Study those legs. You were thunder-thighs back then."

"Give me that." Jennifer grabbed the picture out of her hand. "They're beautiful legs, then and now." She giggled. "I *did* look pretty healthy."

"I wonder where all those rolls of fat went," Lexi commented. "You were certainly a squeezeable-looking baby."

"Mom says she played with me for hours at a time because I was so fun and cuddly. She said that until I came along, her life didn't seem complete."

"My brother Egg tells me that his life was complete *until* I came along and ruined it."

"Do you ever believe what Egg says?" Lexi wondered.

"Not often." Binky shrugged. "Egg's a big old bag of hot air."

When the girls were finished laughing and examining the contents of the box, Jennifer put the photos away to study again later.

The next morning Lexi met Jennifer and Binky

by their lockers. "Have you signed up yet?" was Jennifer's first question.

"For what?" Lexi opened her locker and took out the books necessary for her first-hour class.

"The school nurse is doing free blood-type testing. All we have to do is get our fingers pricked. In a couple of days we can pick up a card that gives us our blood type. Sounds interesting. I'm going to do it."

"I'm not." Binky shuddered. "I don't want anybody taking my blood."

"Even a little drop from the end of your finger? That's no big deal. Besides—I'm no chicken." Jennifer gave Binky a disgusted glance.

"I'll go with you right now," Lexi offered. "I think it would be a good idea to know my blood type."

"I don't want to know about my blood, and I don't want to see my blood. And I'm certainly not going to let the school nurse take blood that I might have a use for later." With that, Binky stalked off.

"Let's go," Lexi said. "We have a few minutes before the bell rings."

It only took a moment to get their fingers pricked and to fill out a small card.

"You girls may pick up the card, which will state your blood type, in two or three days," the school nurse told them.

"That was easy," Jennifer commented as they headed toward their first class. "I don't know what Binky was so worried about."

"Binky's always worried about something. If she didn't have something to worry about, she'd worry!" Lexi pointed out. "By the way, how's the scrapbook coming?"

"My parents are going out again. I've been through everything in that box. I found a few good photos, but tonight I'm going to look in my dad's desk. I know he has lots of pictures of me in there. I think he also has a few of when he and Mom were dating. They'd be fun to put in the album."

Suddenly, Ruth Nelson came skidding up to them, her eyes shining.

"Ruth, what's going on?" Lexi grabbed the girl's arm. "Is everything all right?"

"Everything is perfect," she said, her strangely flat voice sounding almost animated. Ruth was deaf, and although she could speak, her voice did not sound the same as those of the hearing students. "Have you heard the news? My parents are coming back!"

Lexi impulsively threw her arms around Ruth and gave her a hug. "That's wonderful! I know how lonely you've been."

Ruth's parents were missionaries stationed overseas. While they were gone, Ruth had lived in Cedar River with her aunt. Although Ruth liked Cedar River, Lexi knew that she preferred to be with her parents.

"Aren't they going to be missionaries anymore?" Jennifer asked.

"Oh, yes. But they're going to spend a year in the States, and I'll be able to live with them."

"Good for you!" Jennifer, too, gave her a hug.

"Aren't you excited? It's been so long since you've seen your . . ." Lexi paused midsentence. "Ruth, if you join your parents, does that mean you'll be leaving Cedar River?"

"I'm afraid so. I'll have to go to wherever they will be."

"We'll miss you, Ruth."

"And I'll miss you." Ruth looked from Jennifer to Lexi and back again. "You're the best friends I've ever had."

Lexi saw tears welling in Ruth's eyes. "Now don't start crying. This is *good* news, remember? You can come back to Cedar River and stay with us anytime."

At that moment, Binky came running up beside them. "Did you tell them the news, Ruth?"

After Ruth left for her class, Lexi, Binky, and Jennifer moved down the hallway together. "I'm really going to miss her," Lexi commented.

"We all will. I learned a lot about the hearing-impaired from Ruth. Besides that, she's a good friend!"

Binky clapped her hands. "I think we should have a going-away party. I'd like to show Ruth how special we all think she is."

"Great idea, Binky."

"Let's do it."

Binky practically bounced as she walked. "This is so exciting! I love parties! I was afraid the next few weeks were going to be so boring; but they won't be now, not with a party to think about!"

Chapter Two

"Todd's here. Gotta go." Lexi hurriedly finished her orange juice, gave her little brother Ben a pat on the head, and waved at her mother as she dashed to the door. She swung a jacket over her shoulder and hoisted her book bag into her arms.

Lexi smiled at Todd as she slid into the front seat of his refurbished vintage car. "Sorry you had to wait. I accidently turned my alarm clock off this morning. If Ben hadn't noticed that I hadn't taken my shower when he went to take his, I might still be sleeping."

"It's okay," Todd said. "We have plenty of time. We're going to stop at my brother's place. I left a book there last night and it's due at the library this morning."

"How's Mike doing?" Lexi recalled her conversation with Binky and Jennifer.

"About the same. He wants Nancy's life—however much of it is left—to be the best that it can be, and he's working hard to make that happen." Lexi and Todd both knew that Nancy was living on borrowed time. She had been diagnosed as having full-blown AIDS; yet, so far she had remained relatively active and productive.

"It must be terrible to think about your death all

the time," Lexi commented softly. "I don't see how Nancy could help but do that."

"Nancy's not afraid of dying. She's a Christian and knows that she's going to heaven. It's just that she doesn't want to leave Mike quite yet."

"Let's talk about something happier," Lexi suggested. "Did you know that Ruth is going to live with her parents? They're coming back to the States."

"That's great! Is she excited?"

"Of course. Binky wants to have a big party for her. In fact, I talked with Binky on the telephone last night, and that's all she had on her mind."

"Binky? With a one-track mind? No way!" Todd joked. They both knew how intense Binky could be.

"Just remember that I warned you when she grabs you in the hall and insists that you help plan the party."

Todd pulled into the parking lot of the Cedar River High School. He stopped the car and pulled the key from the ignition. As they walked toward the school, Jennifer Golden came around the corner.

"Good morning, Jennifer," Lexi greeted her friend.

"What's good about it?" Jennifer growled. She stalked toward the door of the school, head down, shoulders hunched. She didn't wait for Todd and Lexi to catch up as she threw open the door to the school and went inside.

Todd whistled. "She's in a bad mood today."

"That's odd," Lexi remarked. "Something must have happened."

Todd held the door open for Lexi and they stepped into the school. Egg McNaughton was ambling down the hallway; his long, skinny frame looked more like that of a scarecrow than a human body. He stooped to pick up a book that Jennifer had dropped on the floor in her hurry. "Don't forget your chemistry book," he told her. "After all, it's your favorite subject."

"It's not my favorite subject. Give me that." Jennifer grabbed the book out of his hands and stuffed it into the pile she was carrying.

Egg put his hands on top of his head. "I think I'd better hold this on," he commented, "before you snap it off."

"Don't get smart with me today, McNaughton. I'm not in a good mood."

"So I noticed."

"Here, put my books in my locker." Lexi thrust her books into Todd's arms. "I'll go rescue Egg."

Lexi sauntered up to the pair as they glared at each other. "Come on, Jennifer." Lexi touched the girl's arm. "Walk with me to the nurse's room. We have to pick up our blood-type cards today."

"Oh, yeah. I forgot." Jennifer stomped down the hall to her locker, shoved her books behind the metal door, and slammed it shut. "Well, what are we waiting for? Let's go."

Lexi rolled her eyes at Todd and gave him a smile. Whatever was on Jennifer's mind had certainly put her in a foul mood. With a little patience, Lexi might be able to tease or talk her out of it.

There were several students waiting at the nurse's station. The line dwindled quickly, and shortly Lexi and Jennifer picked up their envelopes. Lexi peeked into hers first. "According to this, my blood type is B positive," she said. "I guess that doesn't surprise me. That's what my mother's blood type is, too."

"My mom is A positive. I remember her telling me that once. I'm not sure what type of blood Dad has. Something like A negative. I can't remember." Jennifer pulled the card out to look at it. "It says here that my blood is . . ." Jennifer's voice trailed away. She stared at the card with such intensity that Lexi half expected it to combust from the burning gaze directed at it. She crumpled the card and stuffed it into her pocket.

"Don't you want to save it?"

"What for? I've already read it." Jennifer's strange mood quickly became stranger yet. Though she tried to be nice as they returned to their lockers to get their books for first-hour class, it was obvious that something had upset her.

Lexi glanced at the clock on the wall. Only one minute until class time. This was neither the time nor the place to discover what was bothering her friend. With a sigh, Lexi decided to question Jennifer when she had the opportunity.

———

Lexi didn't see Jennifer again until noon when she carried her lunch tray to the table where she and her friends normally sat. Jennifer and Matt Windsor were already there, as were Egg, Binky, Todd, and Peggy Madison. Binky had a notebook in her hand and appeared to be conducting a meeting.

"Come on, Lexi! Hurry up. You're late. We have to plan Ruth's party."

"Do we have to do it today?"

"There's no time like the present. That's what my dad always says."

"He says that about cleaning your room, Binky."

"I don't see why it can't apply to this situation, too. We don't know how long Ruth will be in school before her parents come to get her. Now then . . ." Binky poised the pencil over her notebook. "Let's start with the very most important thing. What kind of food should we have?"

"I don't care what kind it is," Egg said, "just so there's lots of it. How about pizza?"

"We always eat pizza. That's so boring."

"Then let's order one of those six-foot-long submarine sandwiches from the sub shop."

"How about cake? Who wants to bake a cake?"

"I'm not eating a cake any of you guys make," Matt announced.

"If you think you're so smart, *you* do it."

"All right, I will. I'll order one from the bakery."

"Make sure they write "Goodbye, Ruth, We'll Miss You" in frosting across the top of the cake," Binky ordered.

"Bossy!" Matt muttered under his breath.

"Who wants to have it at their house?" Binky asked.

"I'll ask my mom," Peggy offered, "but I'm not making any promises."

"Great." Binky checked another item off her list. "You can be in charge of decorations, too. Balloons, maybe, and streamers."

"Are you sure you don't want me to pitch tents and have a band in the backyard?" Peggy asked sarcastically.

"You don't need to go to that much work." Binky ignored the teasing.

"Is this going to be a surprise party?"

"Do you think we can keep it a secret?"

"We'll have to be careful," Peggy pointed out. "We won't be able to discuss it when Ruth is in the room. After all, she can read lips."

"I think we can manage that," Lexi commented.

"Egg and I will make up invitation lists." Binky volunteered her brother for the task.

Egg opened his mouth to protest and then closed it again, realizing that it would be of no use. When his sister was in one of her organizing moods, there was no stopping her.

"I've got a great idea," Binky announced. "Let's go to the mall after school today to help Peggy pick out decorations for the party."

"I can't go today," Peggy said. "Why don't the rest of you do it? Choose whatever you want. It will be fine with me."

"How about it?" Binky eagerly turned toward Jennifer.

"I can't." The expression on Jennifer's face had grown grimmer as she'd listened to the conversation swirling around her. "I have something important to do after school."

"Oh." Binky looked disappointed.

"I'll go with you, Binky," Lexi offered. "The two of us can pick out decorations. If we buy something that Peggy or Jennifer doesn't like, we can always take it back."

Binky brightened. "Great." She glanced at the clock on the wall. "I'd better hurry, or I'm never going to get my books exchanged before class."

Everyone stood to leave except Jennifer, who remained seated at the table staring silently at her folded hands. She had tuned out the rest of the group and was left in a world of her own.

——————

After school, Lexi and Binky took the bus to the mall. As they walked to "Parties For Less," which carried party favors, balloons, streamers, and ribbons, Binky brought up the subject of Jennifer.

"She's been in a really weird mood lately. Frankly, she's getting on my nerves. What makes Jennifer think she has the right to be crabby and to insult the rest of us all the time? We all have bad moods sometimes."

"Maybe she's worried about the gift for her parents' wedding anniversary. She's certainly talked about that enough lately."

"That's no reason to be crabby, Lexi. Jennifer should have to live with my brother Egg for a while. Now *there's* a reason to be crabby."

As they turned the corner, the girls saw Minda Hannaford and Tressa Williams standing in front of the window of a department store.

"Oh, it's you," Tressa greeted them. She raised a hand limply into the air in a halfhearted greeting.

Lexi and Binky weren't happy to see *them*, either.

Minda and Lexi had experienced many ups and downs since Lexi had moved to Cedar River. Minda and her friends belonged to a club called the Hi-Fives. They were considered the popular, trend-setting girls at Cedar River High and had consciously excluded Lexi from their group. Still, there had been times when Lexi and Minda were almost able to talk like friends. Lexi had decided long ago to accept Minda just as she was. Minda would never be her best friend, but if Lexi could somehow keep Minda from becoming her enemy, at least they could coexist in the same school.

"How did you get here so fast?" Binky asked. "We came on the first bus."

"I had my car at school, of course."

"I wish I had a car. Dad said I have to earn enough money to buy one. I guess that means I'll be fifty years old and still pedaling around on my bike or taking the bus."

As Binky spoke, Tressa Williams openly studied Lexi. She obviously had something on her mind.

"How's Nancy?"

Lexi didn't feel like discussing Mike Winston's fiancée right now, but it appeared she had no choice.

"Pretty well, I think."

Tressa, who didn't care a shred about others' feelings, snapped her gum and said, "So, is she like . . . dying, or what?"

"I suppose anyone who has AIDS expects death sooner or later," Lexi said quietly. "But she's not dying today, and probably not tomorrow. She feels fairly well and is doing as many speaking engagements as possible."

"It's a real bummer, isn't it?" Tressa continued. "They're not still getting married, are they?"

"They've called the wedding off."

"It blows my mind to think that I know someone with AIDS." Tressa snapped her gum and stuffed her hands into her pockets.

"Come on, Tressa. We have to get going." For once, Minda was tactful, sensing that Lexi was in no mood to discuss this topic further.

After they had disappeared down the sidewalk, Binky put her hands to her head and pulled on her hair in mock fury. "Tressa Williams drives me absolutely wild! What business is it of hers how Nancy's feeling?"

"Nancy's chosen not to be private about her disease, Binky. She wants kids to be aware she's ill, and to think about what can happen to them if they don't make smart choices. I don't think Nancy would mind Tressa's asking about her."

"Maybe not. But I do."

Before Binky could say more, Lexi pointed to a brightly decorated store window. "Forget about Tressa. She doesn't matter. You know that." Suddenly neither felt much like planning a party. Silently they entered the store filled with gaily colored streamers, mylar balloons, and party favors of every kind.

———

"We got a lot of great stuff, didn't we?" Binky's arms were full of packages when they left the store. "What time is it?"

"Almost five-thirty. If we hurry, we can catch the bus. Let's stop at Jennifer's house and show her the decorations."

"Ooh. These packages are getting heavy," Binky complained as they neared the Goldens'. "I'll be glad to get to Jennifer's. I need a rest."

Jennifer's mother answered the door. She had been crying. Lexi could see Mr. Golden pacing back and forth in the kitchen at the far end of the house.

"We came to show Jennifer the decorations we bought for Ruth's party. If this is a bad time . . ."

Mrs. Golden's eyes were red and puffy. Tears made tracks down her cheeks through her makeup. She hesitated for a moment, and then opened the door widely. "Come in, please."

"We . . . we could come back later," Binky offered.

"No. I think you'd better come inside. Jennifer's in desperate need of friends right now." Mrs. Golden took the packages from the girls' arms and set them on the floor by the door. "She's upstairs in her room. Please go up. See if you can talk some sense into her."

"Sense? About what—?" Lexi jabbed Binky in the side with her elbow and Binky closed her mouth.

"Come on, Binky, follow me."

"What do you think she meant by that?" Binky whispered when they reached the top of the stairs.

"I have no idea. I think we'd better find out from Jennifer."

Lexi walked quickly to Jennifer's room and knocked on the door.

"Go away." The voice on the other side of the door was muffled.

"Jennifer. It's me, Lexi. Binky's with me."

"Go away."

"Your mom said we should come upstairs. She said you needed friends. Well, we're here."

"What makes you think she knows anything about what I need?"

Lexi ignored Jennifer's tone. She turned the knob, opened the door, and stepped inside. Jennifer was lying on the bed, her head at the foot, her feet propped on the pillows. Used tissues littered the floor. Her face was streaked with tears.

More frightening than the tears, however, was the way Jennifer trembled. She shivered so that the bed shook.

"Jennifer, what's happened?"

"I don't want to talk about it."

"You're as cold as ice."

"Leave me alone."

Lexi disregarded Jennifer's order, pulled a quilt from the foot of the bed, and wrapped it around her friend's shoulders. "You look terrible. How long have you been crying?"

"Too long."

"Your mother's crying, too. Is somebody sick? Did somebody die?"

"Sort of," Jennifer said enigmatically.

"How can someone 'sort of' die?" Binky asked. "They either died or they didn't."

"I can't talk about it."

"Give yourself some time," Lexi advised. "We can wait."

"I'll never be ready to talk. Never." Jennifer burst into heart-wrenching sobs.

As Lexi soothed Jennifer, Binky paced around the room, stopping occasionally to touch something—a dried corsage Jennifer had saved from a school party, the stack of tapes she prized so highly, and finally, the open scrapbook of her parents' thirty years together that Jennifer had lovingly created.

"This looks good," Binky commented as she pointed to the scrapbook. "It's almost done."

Jennifer flinched as though she had been struck. "I'm never going to finish it."

"But you were so excited about their anniversary. . . ."

"That was before I got the blood test."

"Huh?" Binky looked at Jennifer blankly. "What's that supposed to mean?"

"When I picked up my blood-type card in school

this morning, I thought it was weird that I would have Type AB blood."

"Why? Lots of people have Type AB blood."

"Yes, but their parents aren't both Type A. That's impossible, you know."

"I don't get it." Binky sat down hard on a chair across from Jennifer. "What are you saying?"

"I'm saying that parents who both have Type A blood can't give birth to a child with Type AB blood."

"Then there must be some mistake. People make mistakes all the time. Look at me. I'm practically a walking mistake. Don't worry about it. Just go talk to the nurse tomorrow."

"That's not all." Jennifer's gaze fell on the open scrapbook pages. "When my folks left last night, I went to Dad's desk to look for more photos. There wasn't much there except for an old file at the back of the drawer. In it was a letter from my dad's sister, talking about me and what a beautiful baby I was."

"What's wrong with that?"

"Nothing, except that Aunt Ellen talked about the day I came to live with them. She never mentioned the day I was 'born' or my 'birth day.' She said things like 'the day Jennifer came to live with you was a fresh start.' Don't you think that sounds strange?"

"It's hard to say, not knowing your Aunt Ellen. I suppose you could ask your parents about it."

"I did. Tonight. After school. I told them about the pictures I was looking for. I said I must have been an awfully big baby since there wasn't a photo of me as a tiny baby anywhere to be found. I told them about the blood tests and the letter from Aunt Ellen."

"And?"

"And when I finished talking, my mother looked at me for a long, long time. Tears started to run down her cheeks. She started sobbing. Dad put his arms around her and told her not to cry. I've never seen her break down like that before," Jennifer murmured. "And I hope I never see it again."

"Why was she crying?" Binky's compassionate little face creased with worry.

"She said she'd hoped I'd never find out."

"Find out what?" Binky was getting impatient. "Get on with this story!"

Jennifer's expression hardened. There was a frightening bleakness in her eyes. "She hoped I'd never find out that I'm adopted."

"You're *adopted*?" Binky's eyes grew round. "Wow!"

"Are you *sure*? Maybe there's been a mistake. . . ."

"There's no mistake. I'm adopted. Their dark little secret is out."

"Is that so terrible? Other kids are adopted."

"Don't you see? They *lied* to me. They let me believe that I was their natural birth-child. They kept secrets from me. I don't belong to them." Bitterness punctuated Jennifer's words. "I don't even know who these people are anymore!"

"Of course you do. You've lived with them all your life. What difference is this going to make?"

"Plenty. I don't know my real mother."

"Why didn't they tell you that you were adopted?"

Tears brimmed in Jennifer's eyes. "Mom said she'd planned to tell me, but it never seemed the time was quite right. Finally I got so old that they decided the news might be too difficult for me to handle.

Rather than tell me that I wasn't their biological child, they just hoped it would never become an issue. They lied, Lexi. They *lied*."

"They weren't trying to hurt you, Jennifer," Lexi pointed out. "They were trying to protect you. After sixteen years, they probably thought the news would be too much of a shock."

"I can't believe this is happening to me." Jennifer swung her feet off the bed and gripped the edge of the mattress until her knuckles whitened. "And I never suspected for a minute!"

She jumped to her feet and went to the mirror. "I should have guessed. I don't look like my mother, and I certainly don't look like my father. I don't belong here. I'm not part of this family."

"But you *are*, Jennifer. Your parents are absolutely crazy about you. You know that."

"Then why did they keep the truth from me? Were they worried I'd want to find my real parents? Were they afraid that I wouldn't love them anymore?"

"Look at how you're acting," Binky pointed out bluntly. "Maybe that *is* what they were afraid of."

Jennifer paced the floor. "I can't believe it. *I'm adopted*. I don't belong here. I don't belong anywhere."

"Jennifer, this is your home, where you grew up. . . ."

"I don't know *who* I am anymore." Jennifer didn't seem to hear Lexi's voice or recognize her friend's attempt to comfort her. "This is impossible." Jennifer shook her head in bewilderment. "I can't believe it's true. There must be a mistake. I wish this were just some kind of huge joke that Mom and Dad were playing on me." Her voice trailed away. They all knew this was no joke.

Lexi's mind whirled. It was too much to comprehend. She couldn't begin to imagine how Jennifer must be feeling.

Jennifer sat down on the bed and stared fixedly at a spot on the wall. "Who am I, do you think?"

"You're Jennifer Golden, of course."

"No, I'm not. Not anymore. That's who I was before I found out the truth."

"You're *still* Jennifer. Nothing has changed."

"*Everything*'s changed. My parents aren't really my parents. My home isn't really my home. They lied to me. They made me believe that I was someone that I'm not. I don't know who I am anymore."

Lexi could hear the utter despair in Jennifer's voice.

"How would you feel, Binky, if you had been rejected by your parents?"

"Your mom and dad didn't reject you."

"The Goldens lied to me, and my birth parents gave me away. I call that rejection." Anger and resentment seethed in Jennifer's words. She flung herself backward across the bed. "Think about it!" she cried. "My adoptive parents *lied* to me. My birth parents *gave me away*. I must be someone really awful!"

Chapter Three

The change in Jennifer's personality was swift and frightening.

"What's wrong with Jennifer lately?" Todd asked Lexi as they walked down the school hallway.

"I said hello to her and she nearly snapped my head off. A few minutes ago when I turned to say something to Egg, she came storming up behind us and yelled at me for talking about her behind her back." Todd's expression was baffled. "We were talking about a basketball game that was on TV last night. Jennifer pounced on me like I was telling secrets about *her*!"

"Just ignore her," Lexi advised. "She's having a bad time at home. . . ."

"Like what?"

"I can't tell you yet, Todd. Jennifer asked me not to say anything for a while. Let's just say that she's sensitive to secrets and unshared information right now."

"That's for sure." Todd grimaced. "I thought she was going to slug me."

"You know Jennifer. She's always been excitable."

" . . . and this time she has something to be excited about." Todd finished Lexi's sentence for her.

"Something like that. Thanks for not pressuring me to tell you what's going on. Trust me, she's having a hard time."

"I'm glad you said something," Todd said. "Otherwise I might have spouted off the next time I saw Jennifer. Now I'll keep my mouth shut."

Before Lexi could say more, Binky hurried up with Peggy Madison in tow. "Lexi, I've got to talk to you for a minute. We need to find Jennifer and set a time to finish planning Ruth's party. Will tonight work?"

"Tonight should be fine."

"I want to get all the details settled. Egg's already worried that we're not going to have enough food."

"Egg could be left overnight in a grocery store and worry about there not being enough food for him to eat," Peggy commented.

"My dad says Egg has a hollow leg. I don't believe that's true. I think Egg's completely hollow, all the way from his feet to his head. That's why it takes so much food to fill him up, and he's such an airhead besides. Lexi, will you find Jennifer and tell her that we're planning to meet after school?"

"Sure. Let's meet in the *Cedar River Review* room."

Lexi glanced up and saw Jennifer standing in the doorway of a classroom, but Jennifer turned away before Lexi could wave her down. "Oh, well. I'll catch her later."

Though Lexi kept an eye out for Jennifer for the rest of the afternoon, she didn't run into her again. She even took a tour of the classrooms on the far side of the building before returning to the *Cedar River*

Review room, where Peggy and Binky were waiting for her. "Jennifer didn't come in here, did she?" Lexi asked.

"I haven't seen her all day."

"Did you tell her about our meeting?"

"No. I couldn't find her. I wrote a note and stuck it inside her locker, but I'm not sure that she'll find it before she goes home."

Binky glanced at her wristwatch. "I guess there's no point in waiting for her to come, then. Why don't we make our plans and call her tonight with the details. She won't mind, will she?"

"She'll probably be happy that we did it for her," Peggy commented.

Binky opened her notebook. "We'll start by discussing the food. It's always the most important part of any party."

At that moment the door flew open so hard it slammed against the wall behind it. Jennifer stood framed in the doorway, her face flushed and angry.

"There you are . . ." Lexi began.

Jennifer didn't let her finish. "What are you trying to do? Sneak around my back and plan the party without me?"

"Of course not," Binky answered her. "Lexi tried to find you all day."

"Well, I certainly wasn't hiding." Jennifer's face and tone were so filled with fury that Lexi was alarmed. "Big deal—putting a little note in my locker. It was only an accident that I saw it. I *told* you I wanted to be in on this party."

"And you are. Why are you so upset?"

"You were trying to avoid me."

"Don't be ridiculous."

"You planned all along to meet without me! If you don't want me involved in the party plans, you'd better just say so. I guess I was stupid to think that you actually *wanted* me to help you with this, but Ruth and I are friends, too, you know. It's not fair to go sneaking around behind my back."

Lexi, Peggy, and Binky stared at her. Jennifer's face was red. She clenched and unclenched her fists as she spoke. "I thought you were my friends!" The tears that had welled in her eyes began to stream down her cheeks. "Some friends you are."

The three girls were too stunned to speak. They watched as Jennifer seemed to come apart before their eyes. Binky was the first to gather her composure.

"You're not being fair! We didn't plan this meeting without you. We have been looking for you all day long."

"That's a likely story."

Jennifer's cutting remark caused tears to well in Binky's eyes, too. "Jennifer Golden—you have to know that we wouldn't hurt you for the world. We're your friends!"

"I don't like being left out, and I don't like people doing things behind my back."

"Are you accusing us of keeping secrets from you?"

"What does it look like?"

Binky balled her fists, settled them on her hips, and glared through her tears at the girl across from her. "We don't have secrets from each other, Jennifer. We never have and I hope we never will. The last thing any of us intended to do was to leave you out of this meeting. Frankly, I'm furious that you'd even think those things about us. We're the best friends you've got, and if you want to keep it that way, you'd better start treating us with a little more respect."

Lexi and Peggy watched the whole exchange in mute amazement. As Binky's words sank into Jennifer's consciousness, some of the ruddy color began to leave her face. "Maybe you *didn't* leave me out intentionally. I'm sorry. It just looked that way to me."

"Well, look again. We want you at this meeting. And I think you're really mean, Jennifer Golden, to say all those things to us. Mean and hateful and cruel!"

Jennifer slumped against the wall. "I'm sorry. I really am. The idea that you guys were meeting without me just made me crazy, that's all."

Jennifer closed the door behind her and moved into the room. Silently she dropped into a chair and put her head in her hands. Lexi, Peggy, and Binky stared at her. Binky still looked shaken from the encounter. Finally Jennifer raised her head.

"Ever since I learned I was adopted," she said softly, "I've been wondering if *everyone* is lying to me."

"We'd never do that."

Binky reached to pat her friend on the shoulder. "You can count on us."

"Can I? I don't know who I can count on anymore."

Binky looked hurt.

"Oh, don't look that way, Bink," Jennifer pleaded. "You have to understand how I feel. If my own *parents* could lie to me, could hide from me something as important as being adopted, then anyone could."

"Just because someone kept a secret from you once doesn't mean that people are keeping secrets from you all the time, you know."

"Probably not, but I can't help feeling suspicious."

"You can't second-guess the whole world forever, Jennifer," Peggy pointed out.

"I feel like such an outcast! When I walked in here and saw you together without me, I couldn't handle it. I want to be part of your group, just like I wanted to be part of my own family. But I don't have a family anymore."

"No matter what else is going on in your life, Jennifer," Binky said, "you had better get it through your head that we *are* your friends, not your enemies. You can count on us anytime and for anything. Got that?"

Jennifer's lips trembled. "I thought that about my parents once, too, Binky. Don't you understand why it's so hard for me to trust? The parents I thought were my real parents aren't. And my birth parents gave me away because they didn't want me. How would you feel if you knew you weren't wanted? Who would you believe in?"

Peggy gave Lexi an anguished glance. Lexi knew exactly what Peggy was thinking. After all, Peggy had given a baby up for adoption and kept it a secret. Even Jennifer and Binky didn't know what she'd done. Lexi knew Peggy was concerned that her baby would someday go through the same painful process Jennifer was experiencing now. Would Peggy's baby, sixteen years from now, be as insecure and hurting?

"I think you should give your mom and dad another chance."

"Which mom and dad? My real mom and dad, or my adopted mom and dad?"

"I think you have to give *Mr. and Mrs. Golden* another chance. You're their daughter. They thought they were doing the very best thing for you by not telling you that you were adopted. Maybe it was a bad choice, but it doesn't mean they don't love you."

"I'm not so sure." Jennifer's stubbornness frustrated them all.

"How can you say that about your parents? They'd do anything for you, Jennifer."

"Anything but tell me the truth."

It was obvious Jennifer wanted to love them; she *needed* to love them, and yet she felt betrayed.

"The minute I discovered I was adopted, I started to think about my adoptive parents in a new way. I can't look at them and see *my* parents anymore. They're strangers who brought me into their home and raised me."

Jennifer's expression turned wistful. A dreamy look settled in her eyes. "I've been thinking about my birth parents. I've been wondering how *they* would have raised me. . . ." Her voice trailed off in thought.

"I'll bet they wouldn't have been so strict with me. Mom and Dad always have so many rules and regulations for me to follow. Now I know why."

"I don't think that has anything to do with your being adopted, Jennifer. We've got rules too. . . ."

Jennifer wasn't listening. She was lost in her fantasy. "I just know my mother was beautiful. I'll bet my dad was handsome, too. And kind."

Jennifer's eyes began to glow. "I've been thinking about it a lot. I'll bet one day one of them will come looking for me."

"*Looking* for you?"

"They'll want to know about me and how I grew up. I'm sure it was difficult for them to give me away. They probably regret it as much as I do. Wouldn't it be great if they found me and we could be a family again? I might even have sisters and brothers somewhere!"

"Jennifer, you already have a family." Peggy's words didn't phase her friend.

"Wouldn't it be neat if my mom or dad were famous and wealthy? My parents could be *anyone*. Maybe my dad's a rock star. Wouldn't that be a kick? I hope they're rich. Then, when we find each other, we could take trips together and really get to know each other."

"Jennifer, are you listening to yourself?" Binky asked.

It was obvious that Jennifer was not. She was staring dreamily into space, seeing visions that no one else saw. "I have this idea in my head that they'll hug and kiss me and tell me how wrong it was for them to give me away and how sorry they've been. They'll probably have roses and presents for me. Won't it be great? I can see it all now."

Jennifer was fully focused on the inward pictures her mind was creating. Lexi, Binky, and Peggy looked at one another in alarm.

"I hate to burst your bubble," Binky began, "but I don't think your dreams are very realistic."

"You don't know that, Binky. My parents could be anyone."

"That's right. They could be anyone," Lexi interjected. "What if they *didn't* bring roses or cry with happiness because they had finally found you?"

"After all, your birth mother gave you away for a reason. Maybe she's remarried and hasn't told her husband that she once gave a baby up for adoption. What if you find them and they don't want to talk to you. Have you ever considered that?"

"Quit it, Lexi. You're trying to make me feel miserable. My birth parents are better people than that. I know they are."

"Mr. and Mrs. Golden are your real parents, Jennifer. No matter how many dreams you have, they're the ones who take care of you when you're sick, who visit your teachers at conference time. Your mom is the one who fixes supper for you every night. Your dad is the one who puts money into a savings account for your college education. *That's* what parents do."

Peggy's anguished face made Lexi say no more. Peggy had left Cedar River to stay with her uncle until after her baby was born. Although there was always gossip, Lexi was sure that no one knew for sure what Peggy had done. Now the memories were all coming back to her with painful clarity. Would this discovery of Jennifer's tear *two* of Lexi's friends apart?

Lexi cleared her throat. "I hate to interrupt, but we *are* meeting to plan Ruth's party. Maybe we should start."

Much to Lexi's relief, Jennifer was willing to tend to business. They quickly made several decisions about Ruth's going-away party.

When Peggy glanced at her wristwatch and announced that it was time for her to go home, Lexi breathed a sigh of relief. She, too, wanted to escape. It wasn't easy being around Jennifer these days.

Chapter Four

"Jennifer, do you want to go with Todd and me to Mike's garage?" Lexi asked. "Mike left his jacket in Todd's car. He needs to drop it off."

Though lately Lexi had felt like avoiding Jennifer, she'd made an effort not to do so. Jennifer needed her friends now.

"I suppose I can," Jennifer grumbled ungraciously in response to Lexi's invitation.

"You don't have to if you don't want to, you know." Lexi was actually becoming accustomed to Jennifer's persistently bad mood.

"I certainly don't want to go home! Anywhere is better than being there."

Lexi could tell by the expression on Todd's face that he was already convinced they'd made a mistake by inviting Jennifer to go with them. Once they were in the car, both Todd and Lexi tried to keep the conversation cheerful as they drove to the garage.

"I talked to Ruth today," Todd said. "I don't think I've ever seen her so excited. She's really looking forward to seeing her parents."

"It must be difficult to have missionaries for parents," Lexi commented, "especially if you have to spend months apart."

"I guess sometimes we take our parents for granted, until we can't be with them. . . ." Todd's voice trailed away as he and Lexi realized that they had ventured onto a touchy subject.

Jennifer sat scowling in the backseat. She crossed her arms tightly across her chest and thrust her jaw forward. Her lip trembled as though she wanted to cry, but she wouldn't humiliate herself by letting the tears come.

"Sorry, Jennifer." Todd glanced in his rearview mirror at the unhappy girl then back at the street.

Being around Jennifer lately was like playing around dynamite with a lit match. A single careless statement could make her explode.

"It looks pretty quiet here," Lexi commented as they pulled up in front of Mike Winston's garage.

"My brother is finally getting organized again. Nancy's illness really threw our entire family into turmoil. At least when Nancy's feeling better Mike has more time at the shop."

Todd led Lexi and Jennifer through the garage to Mike's office.

Lexi was surprised to see Nancy Kelvin sitting behind Mike's desk, looking perfectly at home in the clutter while Mike tinkered with a small motor on the floor.

"What are you doing here?" Todd asked. "I thought Mike was making you stay away so you wouldn't see the mess in his office."

Nancy grinned and leaned over the desk to allow Todd to drop a kiss onto her cheek. She was thin but appeared happy. "I have to check on him once in a while, you know. I've been so busy lately that this is the first time in ages I've been to the shop."

"Are you still talking to groups about AIDS education?" Jennifer wondered.

"Yes, and the response has been absolutely wonderful." Nancy's eyes sparkled. "I've never done anything that makes me feel as good about myself as these speeches. When I gave my very first speech at Cedar River High School, I thought my knees would knock so hard that you'd hear them in the back row. I wasn't much of a public speaker in high school, but the topic of AIDS is something I care so deeply about that the words seem to flow out of me."

"That's just a polite way of saying she talks too much," Mike commented from his position on the floor.

Nancy paid no attention. "Do you want to hear more wonderful news? I've been asked to go on TV and do some public service announcements. Isn't that great?"

"Doesn't it bother you," Jennifer probed, "to have to admit to the whole world that you made mistakes when you were a teenager and that's why you have AIDS?"

"I'd like nothing better than the opportunity to go back and change the way I lived my life," Nancy said fervently, "but it won't happen. I've got to make the best of the time I have left. Fortunately, I've found a way. I feel really good about what I'm doing—educating teenagers, letting them know that they're vulnerable to AIDS too." Nancy stepped from behind the desk and moved toward Mike. When she neared him, she reached down and ruffled his hair with her fingers. "And, Todd, don't tease your brother too much. He's been an absolute doll about all of this."

"Yeah, right. My brother—the doll. How much

will you pay me to believe that, Nancy?"

Mike's eyes narrowed. "Don't you have something to do somewhere else, little brother? Someplace where you can't torment me?"

Todd held out the jacket in his hand. "I came to deliver this. Don't be too nasty, or I might take it home with me."

"I've been looking for that jacket."

"Take better care of your stuff in the future. Come on, Jennifer, Lexi. I don't think I'm welcome here."

Laughing, they said their goodbyes. In the car, Jennifer was silent as Todd and Lexi discussed Nancy and the work she was doing.

"I'm so proud of her, Todd. She's the bravest person I've ever met."

"I'll agree with that. She really cares about other people."

"If I'm ever faced with hard times, I hope I can be as strong and brave as Nancy."

Todd and Lexi were both startled by the sudden sound of choking sobs coming from the backseat. "Jennifer, are you all right?" Lexi turned around. Jennifer's shoulders shook and tears streamed down her cheeks.

"I feel so selfish," Jennifer sobbed, rubbing at her eyes with her fists. "I can't stand it."

Todd and Lexi exchanged a puzzled look. "Selfish? What about?"

"I'm so ashamed of myself, but I just can't help it. It's the way I feel!"

"What do you feel?" Lexi attempted to sort out Jennifer's jumbled statements.

"When I look at Nancy Kelvin, I see a person with a *real* problem. She's got AIDS. She's going to die and there's nothing anyone can do to stop it. That's a *real* problem."

"Yes, it is," Todd agreed. "But that doesn't help us understand why you feel selfish."

"Because I can't quit thinking about *my* problem," Jennifer blurted. "No matter what I do, I can't forget that my parents adopted me and didn't even tell me."

"Your problem is real, too, Jennifer."

"But when you think about Nancy and AIDS . . ."

Lexi reached across the seat and grabbed Jennifer's hand in her own. She gave her friend's chilly fingers a squeeze. "It's okay, Jennifer. We know how upset you are. I'd probably be upset too if I were you. That doesn't mean you're selfish."

Jennifer reached deep into her jeans pocket for a tissue and blew her nose loudly. "I feel like I'm going crazy. I've been riding this emotional roller coaster for days. I'm up one minute and so far down the next that I can't stand it. Everything bothers me. Even little things I shouldn't care about. I couldn't find one of my blue socks this morning and I freaked. I cried. I screamed at my mom. I yelled in the laundry room. Then Mom found the sock I was looking for stuck by static electricity to the inside of a pillowcase. I totally lost it over a sock! Can you believe that?"

Jennifer sank against the car seat. "I'm so confused."

Todd pulled the car to the side of the road and turned off the engine. He swung around in his seat so he could face Jennifer. "That sounds pretty normal to me. It's exactly the way I felt when I heard that my brother's fiancée had AIDS. It didn't seem fair. I resented everyone who didn't seem to have any problems. Our problems seemed like the biggest in the world. For a while, no matter what anyone said or did, I couldn't change my attitude. Give yourself some time to get used to this, Jennifer."

"I don't think there *is* enough time to get used to the fact that I was adopted and given up by my birth mother. I have so many questions rolling around in my mind."

"What kind of questions? Maybe you'd feel better if you talked about them."

"*Why was I given away?* I was a tiny baby, Lexi, and they didn't want me. What could I have done that was so awful? How could anyone do that to a baby?"

"You didn't do anything awful, Jennifer. Maybe they couldn't take care of you. Maybe they were just kids themselves and had to finish school."

"Or maybe I was so bad or ugly that they just didn't want me."

Lexi closed her eyes and sighed. This was more difficult than she'd expected it to be.

"I have no idea of the color of my mother's hair or the color of my dad's eyes. I don't know if they're nice people or horrible. I don't know what my father does for a living. I don't know if I have brothers or sisters."

Lexi glanced helplessly at Todd.

"What if I fell in love with a guy someday and he turned out to be my brother?"

"That's not likely, Jennifer, and you know it."

"Maybe not. But there are some things that are more likely that upset me just as much. What if I have some kind of genetic disease and don't even know it because I've never met my birth parents? I might just fall over dead one day because of something I inherited from them."

"Get real, Jennifer," Todd said bluntly.

"Okay. So that might be a little dramatic. But what if I need my medical history? Who'd help me find it? When I start to have children of my own, it will be important to know if they could inherit genetic defects. Besides, I probably inherited my stupidity from them."

"Your stupidity? What's that supposed to mean?"

"You know, my dyslexia."

"Oh, Jennifer, don't be so hard on yourself."

"Why not? I'm somebody's little mistake. A mistake they tried to hide by giving me away." Jennifer's lower lip trembled. "I wouldn't blame Mom one bit if she wanted to send me away or leave me, just like my birth mother did. Then I'll be even more alone than I am now." Jennifer began to weep. Her hands hung limply at her sides, and tears streamed down her cheeks and dropped off her jawbone onto the collar of her sweater.

"Jennifer, please. . . ." Tears formed in Lexi's eyes.

"I feel like somebody died," Jennifer choked through her sobs. "And it's me. My identity has died. I don't know who I am anymore. I don't know where I come from. I don't know *who* I come from. Everything that I thought made me who I am has changed. Don't you see? Jennifer Golden from Cedar River is gone. Who *am* I?"

Silently Todd started the car, and they drove slowly toward the Goldens' home. In the backseat, Jennifer struggled to collect herself.

"Somebody's home," Lexi pointed out as Todd

pulled into the Goldens' driveway. Soft yellow lights lit the windows. Jennifer's mother stood still as a statue behind the sheer curtains in the living room, staring toward the driveway.

"She's waiting for you, Jennifer, and she loves you. You'd better go talk to her."

"I don't want to talk to her. I don't know what to say."

"Maybe she has something to say to you."

"There's no point. Nothing she can tell me will help."

Lexi was startled by the cold edge to Jennifer's voice.

"I don't know those people anymore."

Without another word, Jennifer crawled out of Todd's car. Lexi saw her lift her head and square her shoulders as she walked toward the house.

Chapter Five

Lexi rolled over in bed and cautiously opened one eye. *9:30* A.M. She stretched and yawned beneath the covers. With a groan she hauled herself to the edge of the bed and sat up.

"Good morning, sleepyhead." Mrs. Leighton stood at the bottom of the stairs, dressed in snug-fitting jeans and an old shirt. Her hair was pulled back in a ponytail. She didn't look much older than Lexi.

"What are you doing today?" Lexi asked.

"Heavy-duty cleaning." Mrs. Leighton swung the vacuum cleaner hose she was carrying. "Closets, here I come."

"I don't like the look in your eye, Mother. The last time you looked like that, you threw out a perfectly good box of stuff I'd been saving."

"Then help me clean and protect your 'stuff.' "

Lexi looked at the sun streaming through the windows and then at her mother's determined face.

"Throw all you want, Mom. I think I'd rather be doing something fun today."

"Suit yourself, but I think cleaning closets *is* fun." Mrs. Leighton picked up the vacuum cleaner and marched toward the closet.

Still smiling, Lexi walked into the kitchen. Her

little brother, Ben, was at the counter in his pajamas, eating cold cereal and watching cartoons. His dark hair stuck up in spikes all over his head. His almond eyes still looked droopy with sleep. Mechanically he raised the spoon to his mouth while staring at the antics of the cartoon characters on the screen.

"Good morning, Ben."

"Hi, Lexi," Ben mumbled sleepily.

"I think you got up too early this morning." Lexi ruffled the already tousled hair.

Ben yawned in response.

Lexi took a cereal bowl out of the cupboard and a spoon from the drawer. She was about to pour herself a bowl of cold cereal when the back door flew open and Jennifer Golden burst through.

Ben looked up surprised. "Hi, Jennifer. You didn't knock."

"Sorry about that, kid," Jennifer said. She pulled up a stool next to Ben's, grabbed the carton of cereal and began to eat it directly out of the box.

"Problems?" Lexi asked.

"Big time."

Lexi tipped her head toward Ben to remind Jennifer of his presence. Lexi didn't want Jennifer to discuss her problem until Ben had finished eating and they were alone.

"Would you like a bowl for that cereal?" Lexi asked.

Jennifer peered into the box. "Sure, why not?" She scooted closer to the counter as Lexi waited on her.

"Why didn't you eat breakfast at home?" Ben asked.

"I wasn't hungry there."

"Are you hungry here?"

"Yes, I am."

"It's not very far from your house to our house," Ben pointed out.

"I know, but I got hungry on the walk anyway."

"Oh." Ben held up his empty cereal bowl. "I was hungry, too, but now I'm not."

"You look like you just got up."

"I did." Ben slid off the stool. He took his bowl and spoon to the sink, rinsed them, and placed them in the dishwasher.

"Ben, you'd better get dressed and feed your rabbit," Lexi reminded the little boy.

"I think I heard his stomach growling before I came inside," Jennifer added.

Ben stared at her in amazement. "You heard Bunny's stomach growling?"

"I'm sure that's what it was. Or maybe a truck going by on the next street."

Ben gave Jennifer a knowing look. "You're teasing me."

"Me? Tease you? Benjamin, have I ever teased you in my whole life?"

"All the time."

"Maybe it *was* a truck and not your bunny's stomach, but I *do* think he's hungry."

"I'll go feed him." Ben looked down at his pajamas. "Maybe I'd better get dressed first." With a grin and a wave, the little boy disappeared from the kitchen, leaving Lexi and Jennifer alone.

"What's going on?" Lexi sat down at the counter across from Jennifer.

"What's *not* going on? That's a better question."

Jennifer rammed her spoon into the cereal bowl with a vengeance.

"Eat first, talk later. You might feel better," Lexi ordered.

Just as the girls finished their cereal, Benjamin returned to the kitchen.

"Did you feed your rabbit?"

"I changed my mind," Ben announced. "I want to stay here and talk to Jennifer."

"I don't think that's such a good idea, Ben."

"Why?" Ben's lower lip came out in a small pout. "She's my friend, too, you know."

"Come here, you." Jennifer held open her arms and Ben walked into them. He gave Jennifer a hug. "You're the sweetest boy I know," she murmured into his silky hair.

Ben looked up at her with glowing eyes. "I know. Lexi tells me that, too."

"This child has no modesty."

"And he hasn't got a very good memory, either. Have you already forgotten that you were invited to play with Mrs. Harris's grandson this morning, Benjamin?"

Ben's eyes grew wide. "I did! I forgot!" Suddenly Benjamin went into high speed. He got his jacket out of the closet and pulled it on. He found a lone baseball cap on the closet door, which he plopped onto his head. "Can I go now, Lexi?"

"Go talk to Mom first, Benjamin," Lexi advised.

Ben disappeared from the kitchen but returned a moment later. He poked his head through the doorway to say, "Bye, Jennifer. Come and see me again."

Jennifer lifted her hand in a wave. Lexi saw how difficult it was for her to smile at the little boy.

"Let's go into the living room," Lexi suggested. "There will be less traffic through there."

Jennifer sprawled across the couch. "I am so mad at my parents I could just scream," she announced dramatically. "They're making me crazy."

"Now what?"

"Matt Windsor asked me to go to the concert in Milltown."

"Really? I've heard the tickets are hard to get."

"It doesn't matter whether they're hard to get or not," Jennifer said bitterly. "My parents told me I couldn't go because the concert is on a school night. They said it was too far to drive."

"Bummer!"

"They're such worrywarts. Matt's a good driver. I'd get my homework done ahead of time. It's no big deal that it's a school night. I always stay up late and they've never complained. Now I'm asked to something special and I can't go."

Jennifer punched her fist into a sofa pillow. "They've no right to control my life like that. No right at all! Matt is my friend. I should be able to go with him if I want to."

"Jennifer, you've always had curfews. . . ."

"If I lived with my real parents, *they'd* let me go." A storm cloud of frustration settled on the girl's features.

"You don't know that," Lexi said.

"My folks have never really understood me," Jennifer continued. "Now I finally know why. It's because we're not even related. They don't understand me because they don't know me. Oh, I can't believe how stubborn they are!"

Jennifer scowled at the pillow she was punching.

"Who do they think they are, anyway? So they adopted me. Big deal. That doesn't give them the right to ruin my life."

Lexi's rebuttal was ineffective against the tirade.

"Ahum." Mrs. Leighton stood in the doorway of the living room. Both Lexi and Jennifer looked up guiltily.

"Mrs. Leighton. . . ."

"Mom, how long have you been standing there?"

"Long enough."

Lexi could tell by the expression on her mother's face that she was upset.

"I apologize for eavesdropping, but I'm not sorry I overheard the conversation." Mrs. Leighton stepped into the room. "Since I did, there's something I'd like to say.

"Jennifer, I realize you're very angry with your parents right now, and although I don't think that anger is justified, you do have a right to your own feelings. However, I believe your parents did the right thing by not agreeing to let you go to a concert out of town on a school night. Had Lexi asked to do the very same thing, I would have said no. I don't believe it's appropriate for teenagers to be driving long distances on school nights for something that's not necessary."

"But Matt has tickets. He gets to go."

"Every family sets their own limits, Jennifer," Mrs. Leighton pointed out quietly. "We both know Matt hasn't always had it easy with his family, either. What works for their family may be entirely different from what works in yours."

"I think my parents won't let me go with Matt because ever since I found out I'm adopted, I've been causing them trouble. My real parents would have let me go to the concert. My adopted parents don't care, not really. They just don't want me to get into any trouble."

"Do you actually believe your being adopted is the only reason you can't go to an out-of-town concert with Matt on a school night?"

Jennifer was silent.

"Think about all the *other* reasons your parents might not let you go."

"They're worrywarts, that's all."

"And justifiably so. What if Matt had a flat tire or engine trouble? What if the weather turned bad and it was difficult for you to get home? They know you need your sleep so you can do your best in school. None of that has to do with being adopted, Jennifer."

"Maybe not, but I still think it's mean."

"I went to school with a girl who was adopted. Her name was Gwen." Mrs. Leighton dropped lightly into one of the living room chairs. "She always thought her parents were trying to force her to do things she didn't want to do. She had the idea that they treated her as they did because she was adopted.

"Once, the music director asked Gwen's mother if my friend would sing at church. Her mother was so excited and pleased that she said yes for Gwen. Gwen was convinced that her mother did this just to show her off. She called herself 'her mother's little adopted prize.' It took Gwen a long time to realize that she actually *did* have a good voice and that the music director was *right* to ask her to sing. She allowed the knowledge that she was adopted to color her entire world. Isn't that what you're doing?"

"It sounds silly when you put it that way, but I

think my decision should be *my* decision, not theirs. After all, they aren't my *real* parents—"

"But they *are*, Jennifer," Mrs. Leighton interrupted sternly. "They're the ones who raised you from infancy. They're the ones who care for you when you're sick or hurt. They're the ones who feed you, provide a home, give you spending money, and buy your clothes. I know your parents, Jennifer. They've devoted their lives to keeping you happy and raising you into a fine young woman. That's what *real* parents do, Jennifer. Mr. and Mrs. Golden are your *real* parents."

"But why are they hanging on to me like this? Why can't they let me live and do the things I want to do?"

"This must be as difficult for your parents as it is for you . . ."

"Ha! They didn't find out they'd been adopted."

"No, but you did, and what hurts you hurts them."

"They're being overprotective."

"Maybe they're terrified of losing you and are holding on to you in the only way they know how. Don't you think they're scared, too? They're just trying to keep you close while you're trying to get away."

"I wish they wouldn't hang on so hard," Jennifer said with a pout. "They're strangling me."

"Tell them how you feel."

"Ha! They'd freak out if I did."

"Are you sure? Don't you think they deserve a chance to hear what you have to say before you decide how they'll respond?"

"I just know what they'll say. I've lived with them

my whole life. They love me. . . ." Jennifer's voice caught on a sob.

Mrs. Leighton sat down and put her arms around the girl. "I'd like to give you a hug, Jennifer, to show you how much I love and care for you. I've often felt that you are a daughter to me, too. Ever since we moved to Cedar River, you've been Lexi's dear friend."

Mrs. Leighton brushed away a blond curl that had fallen into Jennifer's eyes. "I love the fact that you feel you can walk in here, throw yourself down on the couch, and talk to me just the way Lexi might. I'm glad you're comfortable here. I see you as one of my 'almost' daughters."

"Thanks, Mrs. Leighton. I didn't know you felt that way."

"I do. I always have. And I'm sorry I didn't tell you until now. I want you to know that people can love one another even though they aren't related by blood. I love you like a daughter, Jennifer, and I've only known you a short time. Is it any wonder that your parents can love you when they've known you all your life?"

Jennifer dropped her head to Mrs. Leighton's shoulder and sighed.

"Guess I'd better go home," she said finally, her demeanor far more subdued than it had been when she'd arrived. "Thanks for listening." Jennifer looked from Lexi to Mrs. Leighton and back again. "Both of you."

"Thanks for talking to her, Mom," Lexi murmured after Jennifer had left.

"I hope it helped."

"I don't know. I couldn't tell. Who knows with Jennifer?"

"Keep on being her friend and loving her, Lexi. She needs you right now."

Lexi's brain was in a whirl as she thought about what had transpired that morning. Could she really help Jennifer? Could *anyone*?

Chapter Six

In the morning, after church, Binky found Lexi in one of the Sunday school rooms collecting her books.

As usual, Binky was in a tizzy. "There you are. I've been looking all over for you. I was afraid that you'd already left."

"What's going on? Some sort of an emergency?"

"I hope not. I've been worrying about Ruth's party. Do you think we have everything ready? I just *know* we've forgotten something. And I want this to be the best party ever."

"The party should be fine," Lexi said calmly. "After all, Peggy is having it at her house and her mom is helping her to get things ready. Moms know everything there is about putting a party together. You don't have to worry about a thing."

"Then why am I worrying?"

"Because it's your major," Lexi said with a grin. "I shouldn't even try to stop you. Go ahead, worry all you want. The party is still going to be great."

"Maybe I should ask the Madisons if they need my help with anything."

"You and I are supposed to be at the party an hour early to help with the final details. I'm sure that will be enough."

"I don't know how you can be so calm, Lexi. This party is very important for Ruth. We want it to be absolutely perfect."

"It will be." Lexi grinned. "And even if it's not, Ruth will appreciate it. You know that she's not the critical type."

"Are you girls talking about Ruth's party again?" Egg sauntered into the Sunday school room. His hair was brushed into a spike. He wore a light gray suit, a white shirt, and a red bow tie with little brown cowboy boots all over it.

"You look nice today, Egg," Lexi said. "Sort of punk-western, I guess."

"I needed a change. Do you like my bow tie?"

"It's very . . . western."

"I know. I like it, too. I wanted to get cowboy boots to match it, but my dad said no. By the way, I'm checking to make sure I'm invited to this party you're having. Are you sure it's not a 'girls only' sort of thing?"

"You're *not* invited," Binky said.

"Yes, you are," Lexi said.

"Well, which one is it?"

"No."

"Yes."

"No."

"Yes."

Lexi put her hand over Binky's mouth. "You *are* invited, Egg. Don't pay any attention to your sister. Be sure to bring Todd, Matt, Tim, Brian, and Jerry, and everyone else who's available."

"Egg will ruin the party," Binky complained. "He'll eat all the food, then burp and gross us all out. Oh, Lexi, don't let him come to the party!"

"Of course he's coming, Binky. You know that. It's been in the plan all along."

"We'll have to buy some more food," Binky muttered ominously. "Truckloads of food. My brother's a bottomless pit. He could eat warehouses full of food!"

"Everything's going to be great. If I see Egg eating too much, I'll take him aside myself and stuff a dish towel in his mouth until everyone else has eaten."

"You'd better behave, Egg McNaughton, or some night when you're asleep, I'll tiptoe into your room, and I'll—"

Lexi put her hand over Binky's mouth again. "Don't make threats you're not planning to carry out. And please quit worrying about Ruth's party. Everything will be great." *If* . . . Lexi added to herself, *Jennifer doesn't do something stupid.*

———

Binky and Lexi arrived at Peggy's house one hour before the party. The decorations were already in place.

"I love the streamers," Binky said. "And the helium-filled balloons were a great idea! Did you think of it, Peggy?"

"My mom did. She provided the tablecloth and napkins, too. We had some left over from a party last summer when our neighbors moved away."

"It *is* perfect, just like Lexi said it would be."

"I told you so," Lexi said with a grin. "Now tell us how we can help you."

They had just finished their preparations when the doorbell rang and the first guests began to arrive.

When Lexi opened the door, she found Minda

Hannaford and Tressa and Gina Williams on the other side.

"Are we the first ones here?" Gina snapped her gum sharply.

"The very first." Lexi invited the girls inside.

After they had disappeared into the living room, Binky leaned over and whispered in Lexi's ear, "I didn't think they even liked Ruth. What are *they* doing here?"

"I invited them," Lexi said.

"You did? Are you crazy?"

"I didn't want anyone to be left out. Besides that, wherever there's a party, there's a Hi-Five. You know that."

"You're a nicer person than I am, Lexi Leighton," Binky said bluntly.

Their conversation was interrupted by the chime of the doorbell as Egg, Todd, and the other boys arrived. Behind them were Angela, Anna Marie, and several others. Ruth Nelson came last. She looked unsure, not quite knowing what to expect.

"Does she know she's having a going-away party?" Binky asked Peggy.

"I'm not sure. I told her we were having a party, but I didn't exactly say it was for her. I thought it might be nice if she had a surprise."

"Hi, Ruth," Peggy greeted her at the door. "Come in."

"It's nice of you to invite me to your party," Ruth said in her familiar monotone voice.

Peggy put her arm around the girl's shoulder. "This is *your* party."

"My party?" Ruth looked past the group in the living room to the festively decorated table and the walls decorated with "Goodbye, Ruth, We'll Miss You" and "Farewell" banners.

"For me?" Tears welled in Ruth's eyes.

"We're going to miss you when you go live with your parents. You know that, don't you?" Lexi said.

"And I'll miss you." Impulsively Ruth threw her arms around Lexi's neck.

"Are you hugging people?" Egg bounded from the chair in the living room to Ruth's side. "I want a hug, too."

Laughing, Ruth gave Egg a big squeeze. He led her into the center of the party. It was noisy. Everyone talked at once except Jennifer. She stood alone by the punch bowl, filling glasses.

As Lexi watched, Tressa Williams sauntered over to speak to Jennifer. Though Lexi couldn't hear what Tressa said, she knew it had to be hurtful, for Jennifer's shoulders sagged and a sad look filled her eyes.

Gossip traveled faster than the speed of light at Cedar River High. Everyone had heard almost immediately that Jennifer was adopted. Even though Jennifer hadn't kept it a secret, Lexi knew that she'd hoped for a little more time to get used to the idea herself. Lexi suspected that Jennifer's adopted status was the topic of conversation between the two girls. Silently and swiftly, Lexi moved toward the punch bowl. As she neared, her worst fear was confirmed. Tressa was, indeed, grilling Jennifer about her being adopted.

"Doesn't it bother you, not knowing who you are?" Tressa asked.

Jennifer looked as miserable as a fly having its wings plucked off.

"Isn't it weird to think that your real mom didn't even want you? That would give me the creeps."

When Tressa's sister, Gina, joined them, Tressa turned to her sister and said, "We were just talking about Jennifer's being adopted. Isn't it freaky how she just found out now, when she's practically an adult?"

Gina wrinkled her nose and took a fresh glass of the punch Jennifer was mechanically serving. "I can't figure out how a mother could possibly give away her own baby. Isn't that cruel?"

Jennifer wilted before Lexi's eyes.

Gina sipped the punch she had taken. "Maybe your mom was somebody rich and famous. That would be exciting, wouldn't it?"

"Someday your real mother might try to find you," Tressa suggested with ghoulish optimism. "Ooh, that would really be weird! At least then you'd know who you actually look like," Tressa suggested.

Tressa and Gina were relishing their conversation about Jennifer's life while Jennifer stood limp and beaten between the two girls.

"Have you guys listened to yourselves lately?" Lexi demanded. "You're being completely rude. She doesn't need to hear this kind of garbage from you."

"Well, here's Miss Goody-Two-Shoes, telling us what we can and can't talk about," Gina mocked.

"Don't be such a prude, Lexi. We're just trying to imagine what it must be like to be adopted. We're not trying to hurt Jennifer's feelings. You know that, don't you, Jennifer?" Tressa and Gina both turned to stare at Jennifer.

"I guess." Jennifer's voice was soft and injured.

"See, told you so."

"I'm sorry about those guys," Lexi apologized to Jennifer after Tressa and Gina had stomped off.

"I should be used to it by now. Everybody at school is asking me the same questions."

"I don't think you should pay attention to any of them, especially not Gina and Tressa. They always talk first and think later. They probably didn't even realize they upset you."

"Who says they upset me?" Jennifer asked.

"Don't try to kid me, Jennifer. I know you too well. You're ready to cry."

"If I were going to get upset every time Tressa or Gina said something thoughtless, I'd be upset all day long every day of the week."

"That's the spirit! Don't stand here by yourself pouring punch. Come talk to Ruth for a while." Lexi pulled Jennifer into the living room, where Ruth looked up and smiled broadly. She patted the seat beside her to indicate that Jennifer should sit down. Lexi was relieved to turn Jennifer over to Ruth's kind, nonjudgmental care.

A burst of laughter from the dining room caught Lexi's attention. "What's going on in there?" she asked Binky.

"I told you we shouldn't have invited those boys. Now we're going to have trouble."

"What kind of trouble?"

"We're going to run out of food."

"There's a ton of food left in the kitchen."

"Not for very long. Tim Anders just challenged my brother Egg to an eating contest."

By the time the girls reached the dining room, the contest was ready to begin. Tim and Egg sat side by side at the dining room table. In front of each of them Peggy had placed a large bowl of dill pickles.

"You're going to have an eating contest with pickles?"

"I told Egg that I could eat pickles faster than he could." Tim grinned. "Now we're going to see for ourselves who's the champion eater."

"You didn't tell me it was *pickles* that you could eat faster than I could. You just said *food*. There are a lot of foods that are better than pickles." Egg looked a little green himself as he stared into the bowl.

"Pickles, candy bars, hot dogs, whatever. I can eat it faster than you can."

Peggy watched the hands of the grandfather clock in the corner. "On your mark, get set, GO . . ." As Tim and Egg began to devour the pickles in the bowls in front of them, Binky turned to Lexi. "Can you believe it? Look at the way those pickles are sliding down Tim's throat! Tim is so skinny. Where's he going to put all those pickles?"

Tim popped the pickles into his mouth, chewed a few times, and swallowed. His bowl was emptying fast. Egg was eating more slowly. His lips puckered and the skin around his eyes was quivering at the tart taste.

"Look at Egg." Binky giggled. "He can hardly get the pickles down."

A big slurping sound came from Tim's side of the table. With a triumphant gesture, he popped the last pickle into his mouth and it disappeared.

"Ah, delicious." Tim sat back in his chair, satisfied. He rubbed his stomach.

Egg looked at Tim in amazement. "Are you finished already?" Egg's entire face was beginning to pucker now. Pickle juice dribbled down his chin from the corner of one lip. He shivered with distaste. "I don't know how you could eat that many sour pickles."

"Sour? My pickles weren't sour. They were great."

"Are you kidding me? Those are the worst pickles I've ever tasted." Egg shuddered as he pushed the bowl away. "I give up. You win."

Minda, Tressa, and Gina burst into peals of laughter.

"What's so funny?" Egg glared at the girls.

"We got you, Egg! The reason your pickles were so sour is because we poured extra vinegar on them. Don't you like vinegar, Egg?"

Lexi could tell Egg wanted to yell at the girls, but he was having difficulty making his mouth work. "If my lips don't unpucker, it's going to be your fault. Somebody, get me a glass of water."

"Here, take this." Todd handed Egg a glass of punch.

Egg drank it and gave a sharp yelp. "Yech. Pickles and punch don't go together at all. What if my mouth never unpuckers?"

"All the better to kiss you with." Minda batted her eyelashes at Egg. Egg lunged after her, but she slipped away, laughing.

The entire room was laughing, even Egg, now that he was beginning to feel confident that his mouth would not stay in a permanently puckered position. Meanwhile the others were discussing the surprising fact that anything, even a triple dose of vinegar, could stop Egg from consuming more food than any other person on the face of the planet.

Ruth stood up, smiling broadly. "This is the most wonderful party I've ever been to," she said. "I'll

never forget the friends I've made here in Cedar
River. It was hard coming here, being a deaf girl and
not knowing anyone, but you've all been kind to me
and you've made me feel welcome. Thank you for
that. I'll never forget you."

"And we'll never forget you, either." Binky
walked to the buffet in the dining room. She lifted a
box from a drawer and handed it to Ruth. "Open it."

Quickly Ruth tore off the wrapping. Inside the
box was a large pink T-shirt and half a dozen colored
markers. She looked up, puzzled.

"This is your memory shirt, Ruth," Binky explained. "Everyone here will sign his or her name on
your shirt. Peggy's mother will embroider all the sig-
natures so you'll have a T-shirt to wear forever with
our names on it. That way you can't forget us."

Ruth hugged the shirt to her chest. "Thank you.
Thank you."

There was a flurry of activity as everyone signed
the shirt before saying goodbye.

"Ruth, your aunt is here to pick you up," Todd
told her.

Ruth took one last tour around the room to hug
each of her friends. "Thank you," she said, her eyes
shining. "I promise—I'll never forget."

Todd and Egg were the last of the boys to leave.
Soon only Lexi, Peggy, Jennifer, and Minda, Tressa,
and Gina were left. They took down the streamers
and posters and gathered the balloons into a bunch.

"Let's drop these off at Ruth's house," Peggy suggested. "A bouquet of balloons, just like a bouquet of
flowers."

Binky looked at her wristwatch. "I'm hungry
again. Anyone interested in going out for pizza?"

Lexi was a little hungry, too. She'd been too anxious about Jennifer to eat much during the party.

"How about you, Jennifer?"

"I can't. I have a lot of homework to do. You know how slowly it goes for me. I promised to come home right after the party and finish it. My mother would never let me go out tonight."

"I don't get it, Jennifer," Tressa said. "You don't have to listen to Mrs. Golden."

Jennifer looked up, startled.

"She's not your 'real' mother, is she? Seems to me you should only have to listen to your *real* mother."

Lexi and Peggy froze in their spots, wondering how Jennifer would respond.

"I'd rather go out for pizza with you guys than go home and do my homework," Jennifer stated flatly. "But I have to listen to her. Even though she's not my birth mother, she's the only mother I've ever known."

Lexi breathed a sigh of relief. It was the first sensible statement she'd heard her friend say about her adoption.

"Well, I guess if you feel that way . . ."

"I do, but have fun without me."

"Maybe we should wait until another night," Minda suggested.

Lexi looked at the girl in surprise. Minda? Being compassionate? Was it possible?

"We'll pick a night when you can go with us, Jennifer."

Jennifer, too, seemed startled by Minda's thoughtfulness. It seemed very out of character. "Sure. That would be great."

Lexi was grateful to Minda for saving the moment. She followed Jennifer to the end of the walk.

"Do you want company? I can walk you home."

Jennifer stared into the darkness. "I think I need to be alone tonight." Without another word, Jennifer walked away, a small, lonely figure against the night.

Chapter Seven

Lexi met Jennifer at their lockers the next morning. Jennifer appeared tired and pale. The skin beneath her eyes was bruised with shadows. Jennifer closed her locker door just as Brian James sauntered up to her.

"Hi, Jennifer."

"Good morning, Brian."

"I was just wondering . . . ah . . . if you'd like to go to the mall with me after school?"

Jennifer looked surprised. "Me? Why?"

"I'm driving my dad's new car today. Don't you remember? I promised I'd give you a ride in it."

"Oh. That. Maybe another time. Not today."

Brian's shoulders sagged with disappointment.

"But I'd like to sometime," Jennifer added. "I really would. I didn't sleep very well last night. I'm going to go home and take a nap."

"Another time, then?" Brian asked hopefully.

"Great. Thanks, Brian."

After Brian had left, Lexi turned to Jennifer. "Why did you do that?"

"Turn him down? You heard why. I'm tired."

"Brian must really like you. He's awfully shy, you know." Lexi couldn't ever remember Brian asking a girl to go anywhere with him before this!

"Brian doesn't like me. He just promised me a ride in his dad's car, that's all."

"He asked you to go to the mall with him."

"So, we'd probably drive up to the mall, take a turn around the parking lot, and leave again. Big deal!"

"He likes you, Jennifer."

Jennifer shook her head stubbornly. "I don't believe that. Anyway, I don't trust anyone who likes me. I thought my parents liked me, and look what they did to me."

"They adopted you. They love you. That's the awful thing they did to you, Jennifer. When are you going to realize that?"

"I've started to worry when people act as if they like me," Jennifer admitted softly, talking more to herself than to Lexi. "I'm suspicious now. Maybe *everyone* lies. I don't trust anyone right now, Lexi. Not Brian James, not my parents, not myself. How can I?"

"Oh, Jennifer. . . ." Lexi groaned in dismay.

"Don't worry about it. It's my problem. I'll work it out somehow." With that, Jennifer turned and walked away.

The day sped by swiftly. After school, a group gathered around Ruth on the school steps to say goodbye. Ruth gave a squeal of delight when her parents pulled up next to the school building. Quickly she embraced her mother and father with tears of joy and big bear hugs.

"Ruth looks just like her mother, doesn't she?" Peggy commented.

"Don't they look happy to see each other?" Lexi

stared at the happy reunion scene wistfully. She was glad that Jennifer was not outside to watch this. It would be far too painful for her right now.

Jennifer! Lexi's eyes widened. If she wasn't out here, where was she?

Lexi left the other girls excitedly talking about Ruth and her parents. She moved quickly down the hallway. Jennifer had not yet left school. Her jacket was still in her locker. With a determination she didn't feel, Lexi hurried toward the women's rest room. If Jennifer were hiding, that would be the likely spot.

And hiding she was. Lexi found Jennifer in the bathroom, crying as though her heart would break.

———

Lexi and Binky were doing homework. Books and notebooks were spread all over Lexi's bed. Lexi sat in a chair at her desk. Binky lay on her stomach on the carpet beside her.

"Lexi? Are you going to answer me, Lexi?"

"What?" Lexi looked down at her friend. "I didn't hear you."

"You haven't heard me all evening." Binky slammed her book shut in disgust, hoisted herself onto her knees, and stared at her friend. "What's wrong with you, anyway? You're a million miles away. Every time I talk to you I have to repeat myself at least twice. What's going on?"

"Sorry. I'm not a very good study partner tonight."

"I don't care about that, Lexi. You know me. Studying isn't my thing anyway. I just want to know what's bothering you."

"A couple of things I guess." Lexi sighed and closed her book. "Todd says Nancy hasn't been feeling well lately."

"Is it the AIDS thing?"

"Todd says Mike is upset because Nancy won't slow down. She's pushing herself to speak to all the high schools in surrounding towns and tell the students about the dangers of AIDS."

"Maybe she's doing so much because she's feeling better than usual," Binky said optimistically.

"I don't think that's it, Binky. I believe that Nancy feels she doesn't have much time left and that she wants to do all she can while she's able."

"Do you think she might die soon?"

"I don't know."

Tears sprang into Binky's eyes. "I wish there were something we could do."

"I know. Everyone does. Sometimes when I see Mike and Nancy together, I feel as though my heart is going to break for them."

"You said there were two things wrong," Binky reminded Lexi. "What's the other one?"

Lexi sighed and ran her fingers through her hair. "Jennifer, of course."

"Oh, her." Binky was well aware of the problems everyone was having with Jennifer.

"She seems so different lately," Lexi commented.

"Not her usual feisty, loudmouthed self, you mean?"

"Exactly. I'm not used to seeing Jennifer quiet and insecure. She's been so depressed. This is worse than the time she rebelled because she was dyslexic and having so much trouble in school."

"I wonder which is worse?" Binky wondered

aloud. "A depressed Jennifer, or a rebellious one?"

After Binky left for the evening, Lexi went to the phone and picked up the receiver. Quickly she dialed Jennifer's number. Mrs. Golden answered the phone, sounding agitated and upset. Before she could say much, Jennifer picked up an extension in another part of the house.

"I've got it, Mother. You can hang up now."

"I was just going to say something to Lexi."

"I've got it, Mother. She called for me. Hang up."

Quietly and without comment, Mrs. Golden's end of the line went dead.

"I didn't mind, Jennifer. I like talking to your mother."

"You called for me, didn't you?"

"Well, yes, but . . ."

"Then she doesn't need to be on the line."

Lexi winced at the angry tone in Jennifer's voice. "You two have been fighting, haven't you?"

"As usual."

"Do you want to talk about it?"

"No. Stay out of this, Lexi. It's none of your business."

Lexi bit her lip to keep from blurting a sharp retort. "I was wondering if you'd studied for your chemistry test yet?"

"No. I don't think I will, either. I hate chemistry."

Talking to Jennifer tonight was hopeless, Lexi decided. She was far too crabby and upset. "I'll see you tomorrow in school."

"Yeah, right." The line went dead.

Lexi might have continued to sit in her room staring at the walls and pondering Jennifer's predicament if Ben had not knocked on the bedroom door. "Are you done studying, Lexi?" he inquired.

"Come on in, little guy. What do you want?"

"Would you like to play checkers with me?" Ben looked at her expectantly.

"I'd love to play checkers with you, Ben. You're my favorite boy, you know."

"Are you sure *Todd's* not your favorite boy?" Ben asked.

"Benjamin Leighton, you're getting too grown up for your own good! Has anyone told you that lately?"

"Not lately. Tell me again."

They played checkers for an hour. After Benjamin went to bed, Lexi wandered into the kitchen. Her mother was washing the counters.

"Have you been out here all this time?" Lexi wondered. "Why didn't you ask for help?"

"I mixed up some cookie dough to keep in the fridge," Mrs. Leighton explained. "The people in this family inhale cookies like other people breathe air."

"Not just any cookies. Only good ones like yours." Lexi put her arms around her mother and gave her a kiss.

"What was that for?" Mrs. Leighton wondered, surprised.

"Because I love you."

"And I love you. What brought on this wonderful mood?"

"I talked to Jennifer for a minute. Her mom answered the phone. They'd been fighting again. I feel sorry for Jennifer. She's so miserable and mixed up right now."

Mrs. Leighton stopped wiping the counter and

turned to look at her daughter. "I understand that you're worried about your friend, Lexi, but please remember that Jennifer's mother has some feelings, too."

"I know that. Mrs. Golden is a great person. I like her a lot. But it was pretty rotten that they adopted Jennifer and didn't tell her about it."

"The Goldens adopted Jennifer because they wanted to love her, Lexi. It might have been a mistake not to tell Jennifer about the adoption, but I'm sure it was a difficult thing to do. I suppose they put it off when Jennifer was younger, hoping that when she matured, she'd be able to understand. Then, suddenly, too much time had passed and it became far more difficult to bring up the subject. They made a mistake, but that certainly doesn't mean that they love Jennifer any less. They might not have handled things in the best manner, but frankly, I think that Jennifer's being awfully hard on them."

Mrs. Leighton looked at her daughter's sad expression and smiled. "You'll have to understand, of course, Lexi, that I'm speaking from a mother's point of view. Moms and dads make mistakes all the time while raising their children, but that doesn't mean that they love their kids any less. Children don't come with instruction books, you know. It certainly would be a lot easier if they did. My blender and toaster came with instructions and my babies came without any. Seems like a backward plan, doesn't it?" Mrs. Leighton brushed a strand of hair away from Lexi's face.

Suddenly, Ben, in his pajamas, came darting through the kitchen crying. "Benjamin. What are you doing out of bed?"

"I went upstairs and said my prayers. I was all ready for bed when I remembered that I hadn't fed my bunny today." Ben was breathing heavily and flapping his arms. "When I fed my bunny, I left the hutch door open for a minute and he jumped out. Now my bunny's trying to run away!"

Mrs. Leighton and Lexi looked at each other in alarm. Mr. Bunny, fat as he was, was no slouch in the hopping department. He could be halfway across town by now. On the way out the back door, Mrs. Leighton flipped on the yard light. There, standing in the middle of the yard with the door open, was the bunny's hutch.

"Look, Mom. There he is. Over by the shrubs." The fat, furry animal sat in the grass. Even from where she was standing, Lexi could see his little pink nose wriggling and his nearly translucent ears trembling. Bunny didn't like the idea of his being out of his hutch any more than Ben did.

"You go to the left, and I'll go to the right," Mrs. Leighton instructed. "We can't let him hop into the shrubs or we'll never find him."

Cautiously, taking small steps, Lexi and her mother crossed the grass. Ben stood frozen on the back steps, his hands held to his mouth, his eyes wide, watching them stalk the rabbit. The rabbit seemed frozen in time and space as Lexi and her mother approached him. Then with one swift kick, he was off the ground and bouncing. Lexi took a dive and landed on her stomach. She had her hand around the rabbit's midsection. She could feel his furry little paws kicking at the ground beneath him and his heart fluttering rapidly in fear.

Ben squealed from the porch, "You got him! You got him!"

Mrs. Leighton lifted the rabbit out of Lexi's hand and carried him back to the hutch. Ben jumped up and down with glee. "Benjamin, have you learned anything from this?" Mrs. Leighton asked.

"I'm never going to leave my bunny's door open again. Never, ever."

"I hope not. And what else aren't you going to do?"

Ben looked down at his pajama-clad legs. "I'm not going to go outside to feed my rabbit in my pajamas after dark when I'm supposed to be in bed."

"Very good. You learned two important lessons, tonight, didn't you?"

Ben nodded somberly. Mrs. Leighton smiled and took her son's hand. "Come on. I'll tuck you into bed again. This time I hope you'll stay there."

Lexi walked across the yard to stare at the too-fat bunny in the hutch. When Lexi returned to the house, she entered the kitchen and noticed the dish-cloth still lying on the counter. She finished wiping the counters for her mother and turned out the lights.

As she left the kitchen, a strange feeling came over her. Jennifer had been on her mind all evening. Something about the rabbit's escape had sparked an idea in Lexi's mind.

Running away. A current of suspicion ran through Lexi. She had an ominous feeling deep in her bones. Lexi grabbed her house keys and headed out the door.

Chapter Eight

The Golden house was dark and quiet. Lexi almost turned away without ringing the doorbell.

"Coward," she muttered to herself and pressed the bell. She could hear footsteps coming from the back of the house. When Mrs. Golden opened the door, it was all Lexi could do to suppress a gasp of surprise.

Jennifer's mother looked as though she had aged twenty years! There were dark rings beneath her eyes and a drawn, pinched look about her mouth that had not been there before. Mrs. Golden was always immaculately groomed, but tonight her hair was pulled away from her face in a headband and she wore jeans and a blouse that had both seen better days. Lexi knew immediately that Jennifer's mother had been crying.

"Is Jennifer here?" Lexi asked.

"She's upstairs in her room." Mrs. Golden's voice wavered. "That's where she spends all her time."

Impulsively Lexi reached out to take Mrs. Golden's hand and give it a squeeze.

"See what you can do," Mrs. Golden pleaded.

Lexi nodded mutely and started up the stairs. The door to Jennifer's room was closed as if to say

"Keep Out, Do Not Trespass." Gathering her courage once again, Lexi knocked on the door. Without waiting for a response, Lexi turned the knob and stepped inside.

The room was a terrible clutter. Clothes were strewn across the floor. Empty pop cans and pizza boxes were stacked on the dresser. A pile of damp towels was heaped beneath one window. Closets were open and a jumble of clothing had cascaded out. The bed was unmade and discarded stuffed animals littered every other available space. A country western song about lonely and broken hearts was playing mournfully on the radio. Jennifer was sitting on the end of the bed. Whatever she was holding in her hand, she shoved quickly beneath the corner of the bedspread.

"Lexi, what are you doing here?" Jennifer moved slightly to prevent Lexi from seeing what she had hidden.

"I just felt like seeing you," Lexi said, unwilling to express the anxiety she had been having about her friend. "Are you done with your homework?"

"Yeah."

"Did Peggy call tonight?"

"No."

"Did Binky tell you what that crazy Egg did when he was cleaning the garage. . . ."

"No."

Talking to Jennifer was like talking to a blank wall. There was a sadness in her eyes that frightened Lexi. What had happened to her beautiful, laughing friend?

Jennifer glanced at the clock on her bedside stand every few minutes. Was Jennifer hinting that it was time for Lexi to leave?

Lexi had a stubborn streak. Her father had insisted more than once that her stubbornness was at least "a mile wide." Jennifer was trying to get rid of her—which meant that Lexi would not leave.

"Why is your suitcase out?" A big soft-sided bag sat near Jennifer's closet on a pile of rumpled clothes.

"Uh ... I was just putting it away," Jennifer stammered.

"Putting it away? You haven't been anywhere."

Jennifer's eyebrows narrowed over her nose. "It's none of your business whether I've been somewhere or not, Lexi. It's none of your business what I do with my own suitcase, all right? Sometimes you're just too snoopy."

Lexi had certainly hit a hot spot. She wasn't about to be put off now. Lexi walked toward Jennifer's bed. Quickly, before Jennifer could reach her, Lexi threw back the bedspread. Underneath the covers was the treasure Jennifer had so quickly hidden—a bus ticket.

Jennifer made a lunge for the mattress, but before she could reach it, Lexi grabbed the bus ticket and held it to her chest.

"Give me that," Jennifer shouted.

"What do you think you're doing?"

"I'm minding my own business and you'd better start minding yours, too, Lexi Leighton."

"A bus ticket? To Minneapolis, Minnesota? Are you crazy?"

"Give it to me." Jennifer clawed for the ticket, but Lexi stepped out of her reach. "My uncle lives there. I'm going to visit him. That's all. Give me my ticket."

"And what will you do if I don't?" Lexi demanded.

"Call your mom? Tell her that I'm holding on to your ticket?"

"No." Jennifer's hand shook.

"Your mother doesn't know anything about this *visit* of yours, does she?"

"Mother doesn't need to know. She doesn't care."

"She does care, Jennifer. She cares a lot."

"You just don't get it, do you, Lexi?" Tears formed in Jennifer's eyes. "They aren't my real family anyway. They won't care if I leave."

"Jennifer, it would break your parents' hearts if you ran away from home."

"They'll get over it. In a few weeks they won't even remember that I existed."

"Get real, Jennifer. They'd miss a stray cat longer than that!"

"That's how I feel right now—like a stray cat they took in to feed and water. I'm not theirs, Lexi. I'm somebody who accidentally wandered by."

"And you think running away is going to solve all your problems?"

"It might. Nothing else has." Jennifer sank to the edge of the bed and put her face in her hands. "I don't belong here. I don't belong anywhere."

Lexi put her arm around Jennifer's shoulders. They sat there silently, their heads touching. "This looks like a cry for help to me."

"It's a cry, all right. I've been crying for days, but no one comes to help me."

"Go to your parents. They want to be here for you now."

"I don't feel like I belong to them anymore, Lexi. It's the most horrible, empty feeling I've ever known. I'm not theirs and they're not mine. Don't you see?"

"No, I don't. They'd give their lives for you, Jennifer. Don't you *see* that?"

There was a stubborn slant set to Jennifer's mouth that told Lexi that Jennifer was not buying anything she was saying.

"Think about this for a minute," Lexi said. "If you go to Minneapolis, will you go to your uncle?"

"He's not really my uncle any more than my parents are really my parents."

"Do you know other people in Minneapolis?"

"No. We haven't been to Minneapolis very many times."

"How would you find a place to live? What would you do for money? How would you buy food?"

"I've got a little money saved up," Jennifer said bravely.

"How much money?"

"Almost three hundred dollars."

"The last time my dad went to Minneapolis for a convention, he paid a whole lot more than that for a hotel room for a week."

"A week?" Jennifer gasped.

"And, of course, you'd have to eat. Or weren't you planning to eat?"

"I'll get a job."

"Doing what?"

"Waiting tables, baby-sitting. I don't know. Something."

"And that's what you'd do for the rest of your life?"

"Of course not. I'd go to college."

"Really? How would you pay for that?"

"I'd . . ." Jennifer stammered. "I don't know."

"Jennifer, you're trying to hurt your parents by

running away. And you'd do that. You'd hurt them big time. But you would also hurt yourself. You wouldn't feel any better about yourself in Minneapolis. You'd feel the same crummy way you do right now, only you'd be lonely besides. You wouldn't have money, a job, or a place to stay. You'd probably have to go to a homeless shelter," Lexi said bluntly.

"Before you run away, you'd better talk to Angela Hardy. She can tell you what it's like to live in a shelter, to share a room with dozens of other people, to get kicked out on the street in the morning, and not be allowed back into the shelter until night. She knows what it's like to wander from soup kitchen to soup kitchen looking for meals. She knows what it's like to lose everything, and frankly, Jennifer, I don't think she'd recommend it."

"I wouldn't end up like Angela and her mom . . . would I?"

"It seems to me that it would be a whole lot easier to stay here and try to work it out with your parents than to go to a strange city."

"I guess I didn't think this through completely," Jennifer admitted.

"You can run away from this place, but you can't run away from things in your own mind."

"Oh, Lexi. I'm so confused."

"Jennifer, think about what you'd be doing to all the people around you if you ran away. To me, to Todd, to your parents, to Binky and Egg."

"Why would you care?"

"We'd *all* be here in Cedar River, wondering where you were and waiting to hear from you. If something happened to you—something bad—we'd never hear from you again. Don't you think that would affect us for the rest of our lives?"

"Quit it, Lexi. You're trying to make me feel guilty."

"You need to feel guilty. It's a rotten thing you're thinking of doing."

"Then what am I supposed to do, Lexi?" Jennifer choked on a sob in her voice.

"Talk to someone about your problem, Jennifer. Don't try to hold it all inside. If you won't talk to your parents, find someone else who will listen."

"I can talk to you, Lexi."

"I'll listen, but I can't help you any. Find someone who can really help you. Go to Pastor Lake. He's probably had experience with things like this. Talk to Mrs. Waverly, Mr. Raddis, or one of the other teachers at school. Tell them what's happened and ask them to help. You need a counselor. This is too big for you to handle alone. Besides, my mother says that even though sometimes things seem so awful when you're going through them, after a while you can look back and see how much you've learned from the experience. Maybe this will be like that."

"I'm learning a little too quickly, don't you think?" Jennifer weakly joked.

"Your parents are the best friends you have. You need them, and guessing from the look on your mother's face when I came, she needs you."

There was a knock on the door. "Girls, are you all right?"

The door swung open and Mrs. Golden peeked inside. Lexi could see how hesitant and tentative she was about stepping into Jennifer's room. She was as frightened and confused as her daughter.

Mrs. Golden took two steps into the room before

she saw the suitcase open by the closet door. Lexi was still holding the bus ticket in her hand. Mrs. Golden's gaze traveled from the suitcase to the bus ticket and back again.

"Oh, Jennifer. You aren't . . . you're not . . . you can't!" Mrs. Golden rushed to her daughter, tears streaming down her face. "Don't run away, Jennifer. Don't leave us. Give us a chance to work this out together. It would break my heart if you ran away. I love you so much." She gathered Jennifer into her arms and stroked the girl's blond hair gently. "I'm sorry you're unhappy. Your father and I never meant to do this to you. Dad and I will do whatever we can to prevent more unhappiness in your life. Don't run away from the problem. Don't run away from us. We'll get through this together."

Quickly and silently, Lexi left the room. Whatever happened next was between Jennifer and her family.

Chapter Nine

"I wonder how Ruth is doing with her parents," Binky said as she stuffed her jacket carelessly into her school locker. "They must have a zillion things to talk about after being apart for so long, don't you think?"

Without waiting for Lexi to answer, Binky continued. "I hope she likes her new school as well as she liked Cedar River High. It'd be hard to go to a new school, wouldn't it?"

Lexi let Binky ramble. She didn't feel like talking, and Binky didn't seem to notice that she wasn't responding. Lexi's eyes were on Jennifer, who had arrived a few moments earlier. Jennifer was pale and somber. She, too, seemed relieved by Binky's chatter. It gave both girls an excuse for not speaking.

"I'd like to go to a new school someday," Binky announced to no one in particular. "To see what it's like. Then, of course, I'd want to come right back to Cedar River."

Todd and Egg walked up to their lockers to put their books away. Todd looked dreadful. While Binky and Egg exchanged their usual brother-sister banter, Lexi pulled Todd to one side. "What's wrong with you? You look terrible."

"Good morning to you, too," he retorted.

"You know what I mean. You look as though you didn't sleep all night."

"I don't think I did." He rubbed his fingers through his golden hair. His hand was trembling. "Nancy is back in the hospital. My mom and dad spent the night there with Mike. I spent the night waiting for the phone to ring with some news about her condition." He gave a weary sigh. "Last night was the longest night of my life."

"Todd, I'm so sorry. I had no idea. Why didn't you call me?"

"Because I didn't have anything to say. Every time something goes wrong with Nancy, I wonder if this will be the last time. Will she die now? I didn't want you awake all night, too."

"Has there been any word?"

"She's about the same. My folks came home at six A.M. They couldn't get Mike to leave the hospital, but they decided to come home and sleep a few hours.

"I wish Nancy's parents were here to help them out. Nancy's father had a stroke recently, and her mother can't leave him. My mom and dad promised the Kelvins they'd do everything they could for Nancy."

"How *is* Nancy?" Lexi wondered.

"She's very calm. She told my mom that she's eager to live but not afraid to die. She told Mom that she's been remembering that verse in the Bible, 'In my house there are many rooms; I go there to prepare a place for you.' She's sure that there's a place in heaven for her, and she knows that she's going to be happy there. The only thing she's frightened of is the 'trip over.' "

"Do you mean dying?"

"It's the pain of leaving Mike she's worried about, not what she's going to find in heaven."

"Do you really think this is the end?" Lexi dared to ask.

"I have no idea. I don't suppose anyone does."

"Look how well Nancy's been doing. She's been speaking in schools and—"

"She's been pushing herself to her limits and beyond," Todd interrupted. "The only thing that's kept her going is her determination. I've never met anyone I admire more than my brother's girl."

"How's Mike?"

"Calm. It's as though he's finally accepted what's happening to Nancy."

"How does a person accept AIDS anyway?" Lexi wondered. "If I were Mike, I'd be so angry at all the bad things that have happened to them."

"Mike and Nancy think being angry is pointless. He's tired of wishing for what could have been. Now he's just enjoying what is."

Todd glanced at his watch. "I'd better go. I promised I'd talk to the coach for a minute before class starts."

He looked tired and beaten as he walked away. Lexi leaned her forehead against the cool metal of the locker. Her brain was whirling. Jennifer, Todd, Mike, Nancy . . . so much was happening to her friends. Everyone's lives were spinning out of control. Lexi felt overcome with helplessness.

But if Nancy and Mike could be upbeat and positive, then she could, too. Things weren't that bad with Jennifer. At least she hadn't run away.

Lexi decided to be grateful for the small things

these days, because none of the big ones seemed to be turning out very well.

———

Lexi didn't have an opportunity to talk to Jennifer again until after school. She caught up with her as Jennifer was walking toward the front door.

"Jennifer, wait up."

Jennifer hesitated and slowed her stride. She appeared distracted and withdrawn.

"Why don't you come over to my place tonight?" When Jennifer didn't respond immediately, Lexi added, "Please?"

Lexi needed Jennifer's company tonight as much as Jennifer needed hers.

"I suppose."

They'd done this dozens of times, Lexi mused as they walked together toward home, but tonight seemed different somehow. Lexi and Jennifer had shared many problems since Lexi had moved to Cedar River. Yet tonight the problems seemed so much larger and more complicated than they'd ever been before. Neither girl spoke as they turned up the walk toward the Leightons' front door.

"Mom . . . Ben. . . . Anybody home?" Lexi called into the silence.

Lexi led the way through the house into the kitchen. On the kitchen table, a note was propped against a saltshaker.

Lexi, it read. *Ben and I are going for groceries. I'll wash the car and run a few errands. See you before supper. Love, Mom.*

"Are you hungry?" Lexi asked as she put down the note.

"Not really," Jennifer said listlessly.

"How about some popcorn? With extra butter." Lexi popped the corn while Jennifer melted butter in the microwave. Together the girls carried the snack into the living room. Lexi dropped into her father's easy chair while Jennifer perched on the edge of the couch like a nervous bird eager to fly away.

"Sit back and relax, Jen," Lexi ordered. "There's no one to run away from here. Relax."

"I've been trying. It's just not working."

"I feel so helpless," Lexi admitted. "Is there anything I can do that will help?"

"No. Nothing. If there *were* a way for you to help me, I'd tell you in a minute. What I want most is to finish this whole adoption business."

"Finish it? I don't understand what you mean."

"When I discovered that I was adopted, I felt as though someone had died—my birth parents. I felt as though I'd lost someone precious to me. And my other life died too. I don't know who I was or what I might have become if I had been with my birth family. I'm mourning for parents and a life that I never got the opportunity to have. I'd like to put that feeling behind me, Lexi. It's really beginning to get me down."

"How are you going to do that?"

"I don't know. All I do know is that I can't go ahead with my life until I work through this. I feel like someone died and I never had the opportunity to say goodbye to them. Do you know what I mean?"

"It makes sense," Lexi said. "I felt that way when my grandfather died. There were so many things I wanted to say to him, and I never got the chance."

"That's it exactly, Lexi."

"But your birth parents gave you up seventeen years ago. You can't say goodbye now. It's impossible."

Jennifer's expression grew very somber. Her blue eyes were intent. "I've thought of a way."

"What are you saying?"

"I want to look for my birth parents."

"Seriously?"

"What else can I do, Lexi? I've got so many questions running through my mind. It's driving me crazy. I just can't get used to the idea that I'm adopted."

"Looking for your birth parents is a pretty big deal. Are you sure about this? You're opening an awfully big can of worms."

"I need to know, Lexi. Deep down inside of me, I need to know."

"What if you don't like the answer?" Lexi wondered softly.

"You mean if I discover that my birth parents didn't love me and were happy to be rid of me?"

"Something like that."

"Then I'll have to deal with it. I might also find that they loved me so much that they felt they had to give me up in order for me to have a better life."

"I think that's what happened, Jennifer. I really do."

"You think that, Lexi, but you don't really know. That's what I need—*to know*." Jennifer tucked her knees under her chin and wrapped her arms around her legs. She sighed. "I suppose it's not very realistic, but every time I think of my birth mom, I imagine that she's rich and beautiful and that she wouldn't be nearly as strict as my own parents are with me."

"That's your *wish*, Jennifer, not reality. What if you discover that your mother is very ordinary? Maybe she won't even want to see you."

"Maybe she *won't* want to see me. Maybe she's remarried and her husband doesn't even know that she gave me up. Maybe I've got brothers and sisters! I think it would kill me, Lexi, if my birth mother didn't want to see me."

"That's a risk you'd be taking."

"I still can't help wanting to look for them. Just think how many of my questions would be answered then."

"Maybe, maybe not. What if you find more questions than answers?"

Jennifer sprawled across the couch with her head on the pillow. "I know. I've thought about that. That's why I'm so afraid. I've been really angry with my parents—the Goldens, I mean. Even though I haven't been acting like it much lately, I know that they are the best and only parents I've ever known. They made a mistake not telling me that I was adopted, but they haven't made many other mistakes in my life. Mom and Dad are great. I really do love them."

"I'm glad to hear that," Lexi said bluntly. "I was beginning to wonder. I think you'd better tell your parents that, too. Every time I see your mother, she looks like she's about to burst into tears. You've been really hard on her, you know."

"I know. I've been scum. I have all these thoughts and feelings whirling around inside me and don't know what to do about them. Frankly, it's pretty scary to think about looking for my birth mother. What if I create even more problems than we have right now?"

"Then maybe you should leave the past alone," Lexi suggested. "You don't need to see your birth mother. You already have a mother."

"Deep in my heart I know that. But I don't want to live a lie anymore. I don't want my life to be an unsolved mystery. There are too many questions that need to be answered. Ever since I found out that I was adopted, I've been worrying that I wasn't 'good enough' to keep."

"Jennifer, don't be so hard on yourself."

"Don't you think a person should at least know where she was born? At the hospital? In a house? I always thought it was weird that my mom never talked about the day I was born," Jennifer admitted. "Did my birth mom hold me and feed me, Lexi? Did she count my toes and my fingers? What did I do when she held me? What did she look like? I don't even know what my mother looked like."

"Please talk to your mom about this," Lexi pleaded.

"I know. I know," Jennifer murmured. "I have to talk to Mom, but I've been putting it off."

Jennifer reached for another handful of popcorn. "You're lucky, Lexi. You know who your mother and your father are. You know that they love each other. If my parents loved each other, why did they give me away?"

Jennifer rolled to her back and stared at the ceiling. "Why does life have to be so hard, Lexi?"

Chapter Ten

"Have you got much homework left, Lexi?" Mrs. Leighton asked as she walked through the dining room, wiping her hands on a dishcloth.

"Almost done. Every teacher in every class gave more homework than usual today." Lexi dropped her pencil. "In fact, I think I'll save some of this for tomorrow morning. I need a break."

The telephone rang. "That must be for you," Mrs. Leighton said. "It always is in the evenings."

Lexi picked up the phone. "Hello. . . ."

"Lexi, you've got to come over. Now." Jennifer's voice was frantic on the other end of the line.

"What's going on? Is something wrong?"

"Come over. Please?"

"I suppose. But why—"

"I've been trying to work myself up to do this all day. I need you here for moral support."

"What are you talking about?"

"I'm going to talk to my mother about searching for my birth mother. I want to do it, but I need you here when I talk to her about it."

"It's not right for me to be there. That's something very private."

"I need you!"

"I'm sorry, Jennifer. I can't. I'm sure your mom would feel uncomfortable if I were there. I know that I would."

"I can't do it without you," Jennifer insisted. "I'm too nervous. You don't have to say a word. Just be there for me, please?"

"Jennifer, it's too much to ask."

"Then I won't do it. I won't do it unless you come."

"Let me stay out of this," Lexi pleaded.

"Then I won't do it." There was a note of finality in Jennifer's voice.

"You've *got* to talk to your mom. She needs to know."

"Then you'll come?"

"I'm going to get you for this," Lexi muttered. "You owe me one."

"Hurry. Come right now. I'll be waiting for you."

"The things I do for friends," Lexi muttered as she hung up the receiver. "I should have my head examined."

———

Lexi reluctantly rang the Goldens' doorbell. Mrs. Golden answered the door. "Hello, Lexi. How good to see you. Come inside." Mrs. Golden put her arms around Lexi and gave her a hug. Lexi liked Jennifer's mom and felt sorry for her. Lexi hugged Mrs. Golden in return.

"There's something I want to say to you, Lexi," Mrs. Golden began.

Now what?

"Whatever happens, I want you to know that I appreciate your being such a good friend to my daughter."

Lexi had a hunch that Mrs. Golden already knew what was coming.

They sat down together at the kitchen table. Without preamble, Jennifer blurted, "I want to find my birth parents. I need to know about my adoption."

"Ask me anything you like. I'm willing to tell you as much as I know."

Lexi glanced at Mrs. Golden. She seemed surprisingly composed.

"How old was I when you adopted me?" Jennifer asked.

"Less than two weeks old. Your adoption went very quickly because we went through a private attorney. Perhaps that's why, in part, it was so easy to keep from you the fact that you were adopted, Jennifer. You were so tiny when you came to us that it seemed we'd had you forever. You were ours from the very beginning. I know this might seem hard for you to understand, Jennifer, but you are my child. It makes no difference to me whose body you came from. You're mine. I've nurtured you."

"What about Dad?" Jennifer's expression was intent.

"Frankly, he's had a hard time remembering that you're adopted because you've been so much ours for so long."

"Did you forget, too?"

Mrs. Golden shook her head sadly. "No, I didn't forget. Each year as your birthday nears, I think about it." Mrs. Golden's hands began to tremble in her lap.

"Why?"

"Because I think of your other mother. I wonder how it must be to face that day knowing you don't have your child with you. I feel sorry for her. I imagine how painful it must be. Sometimes when I'm alone and it's quiet, I think about how afraid I am."

"Afraid? Of what?"

Mrs. Golden looked directly at Jennifer. "Afraid of what is happening now. I've been terrified that you'd discover you were adopted. I knew that we'd made a mistake not telling you sooner, but we didn't want to share you."

"Share me? What do you mean?"

"I didn't want you thinking about any other mother but me. It sounds selfish, but it's how I've felt for a long, long time. I love you so much, Jennifer, that I didn't want anyone or anything to come between us."

Mrs. Golden had lived with a lie because she was afraid of what might happen if she told the truth. *She was afraid of losing her child!*

"I know how angry you are," Mrs. Golden began, tears forming in her eyes. "But I want you to know that we did everything in our power to be good parents."

"You *are* good parents." Jennifer spoke so softly it was difficult to hear her words.

"Remember this, Jennifer. You are *my* child. It's difficult for me to admit you were someone else's child once."

"Mom, I don't want to hurt you, but I really feel it's important that I look for my birth mother."

Mrs. Golden's shoulders sagged. "I won't stand in your way. All I ask is that you try to understand my feelings. I don't want to lose you, Jennifer."

"You won't lose me, Mom. Not if you let me do this."

Mrs. Golden's eyes fluttered closed and she sighed deeply.

Lexi spoke hesitantly. "You've got to see things from your mom's point of view. If you do find your birth mother and really like her a lot, maybe you'll decide you'd like to be nearer to her. Maybe she will be able to give you things that Mr. and Mrs. Golden feel they can't. Perhaps you'll discover you have brothers and sisters that you want to get to know better."

"I can handle all those things."

"There's another side, too," Mrs. Golden said softly. "If you look for your birth mother, there's always the possibility that she will reject you."

Jennifer winced.

"This is an issue with *many* sides, Jennifer," Mrs. Golden continued. "I certainly won't stop you if you want to look for your birth parents. But, before you do, I would like you to talk to another adoptee who has searched for his birth parents."

Jennifer looked at her mother warily, as if this were a trick. "Who do you know who's been adopted and looked for his parents?"

"Pastor Lake."

Jennifer's eyes grew wide. "Really? Pastor Lake is adopted?" This was news to Lexi, as well.

"When we began having our problems, I needed someone to talk to," Mrs. Golden admitted. "So I went to Pastor Lake. I told him our situation. He explained that he could understand perfectly, because he too had been adopted."

"I don't mind talking to him," Jennifer said, relief in her voice. "He's a friend. He'll be easy to talk to."

Mrs. Golden took Jennifer's hands in her own.

"I'm so glad to hear you say that. I'll feel much better knowing that he's there to guide you and help you through this."

"Thanks for understanding, Mom. You've made this a lot easier than I expected it would be."

"Jennifer, I'll do anything I can for you. Remember that."

Jennifer walked Lexi to the door. "Thanks for coming. I really appreciated it."

"Your mom was great, Jennifer. You could have done this without me."

"I know. But I didn't want to. I don't want to go see Pastor Lake alone, either. Will you come with me, Lexi?"

"Oh, no. Not again. Don't ask me."

"I need you there, Lexi."

"I don't want to be butting in where I'm not supposed to be. This is your private family matter. Besides, there's nothing to be afraid of. You know Pastor Lake just as well as I do."

"I want you to be there," Jennifer insisted stubbornly. "I'm going to ask my mother to make an appointment for us with Pastor Lake after school."

"Jennifer, you're absolutely too much."

Jennifer held the door open for Lexi as Lexi left the house. The last words Lexi heard as she walked down the sidewalk were . . . "Now don't forget, Lexi. You're coming with me."

When Lexi and Jennifer arrived at church, the parking lot was empty except for Pastor Lake's car.

"Are you nervous?" Lexi wondered. "I am."

"That isn't even the word for it!" Jennifer exclaimed. "My stomach is doing cartwheels."

"Mom wanted me to have an afternoon snack, but I told her I didn't dare. I thought I might throw up." Lexi felt nervous, but she was also curious. Until now, she'd never tried to imagine what an adopted child might think or do, or how one would differ from her. Impulsively she grabbed Jennifer's hand and squeezed it tightly.

"It's going to be okay, Jennifer. It really is."

Pastor Lake greeted them as they stepped into the hallway. Dressed casually in jeans and a sweatshirt, he looked very different than he normally did on Sunday mornings.

"Hi, girls. You're right on time. Come into my office." Instead of taking the chair behind his desk, Pastor Lake moved aside a stack of books and sat down on top of his desk. He crossed his arms over his chest. "I'm glad your mother called, Jennifer. I know a little of what you're going through. I had to wage my own struggle to accept the fact that I was adopted."

"You knew about it from the time you were little, didn't you?" Jennifer guessed.

"Yes. Even so, there comes a time when you begin to question who you are and where you came from. That's a perfectly normal and natural occurrence. The time came when I wanted to know more about my birth parents and my heritage. I began to wonder if there were people anywhere in the world who looked like me. Did I have brothers or sisters? Where were they? I've asked every question that you're asking right now."

"I still think that's easier than having this adoption business dropped on you when you're in high school," Jennifer said. "It's blown my mind to learn that I'm adopted."

"Understandably so. But talking about it is much better than holding your hostility and antagonism inside where it can fester and grow. Questioning is fine, Jennifer. Every human being has questions about some part of their life sooner or later."

"Tell me what it was like for you, Pastor Lake."

Pastor Lake smiled at Jennifer's eagerness. "I was twenty-one years old when I met my birth mother. My parents helped me to find her. When I look back at it now, I'm glad they did. Otherwise, I might have blundered in upon the poor woman with my clumsy questions and terrified her."

"Why do you say that?" Jennifer looked puzzled.

"Imagine how a woman might feel if she received a call from a child she had given up for adoption twenty plus years before. A lot of things would have happened in that time. Perhaps she'd married and had other children, started a new life, tried to put the birth of that baby behind her. Maybe she'd even made the decision never to mention that child's birth to her new husband. How would she feel if a bumbling twenty-one-year-old came stumbling into her life and exposed all that she had worked to conceal?"

"I never thought of it that way."

"I didn't either, but my mother did. After the search, when I had my birth mother's name and number, my mother offered to make the call to my birth mother for me. I thought I wanted to do it myself, but when it came right down to it, I was so nervous and afraid of being rejected again that I let her make the call.

"Later, I was grateful. Mom was very kind and

very gentle. She explained to the woman that she was the mother of an adopted son. She said she believed the party to whom she was speaking was her son's birth mother. She gave some details about me that only my birth mother would have known, and asked her if she would like to meet me."

"As it turned out, my birth mother had married and had a family, but she'd never told anyone about the child she had given up. Still, she was curious and anxious to meet me. We arranged a time and a place. It was very strange. I remember the moment as if it were yesterday. I walked into a restaurant and there she was, sitting in the far corner of a booth. I knew immediately that she was my mother. My hair is the same color as hers. My prominent cheekbones are the mirror image of her own."

"What did she say to you?" Jennifer asked.

"Not a lot. We were two strangers meeting for the first time. The only thing we really had in common was our genetic makeup. Still, I could see in her expression that she was as curious about me as I was about her. We visited for a little while. I told her I was in college and planning to become a minister. That seemed to please her a great deal. When we parted, she asked me to give my mother a message. She said, "Tell your mother that she did a wonderful job raising you. She should be proud." Lexi could see tears welling in Pastor Lake's eyes as he remembered that emotional moment.

"That's it? That was all?" Jennifer asked.

"It was enough," Pastor Lake replied. "She also gave me a typed list of family illnesses and medical histories. She cried a little when she told me that one of her gifts to me was a 'healthy family tree.' It was very comforting to me. It's nice to know there are no genetic time bombs ticking inside my body."

"Did you want to get to know her better?"

"No, not really. My mother and dad were the only parents I'd ever known. My birth mother was just that. My *birth* mother. She was there for my birth. She was not there for my life. She'll always have a special place in my heart, Jennifer, but she'll never replace my parents."

Shivering in the warm room, Jennifer hugged herself with her arms. "It scares me. What if my birth mother doesn't want to see me? What if she thinks I'm going to ruin her life? What if she hates me?"

"It's not likely that she hates you, Jennifer. She might have given you up for any number of reasons. Perhaps she didn't have the money to raise you, or was very, very young—little more than a child herself and couldn't raise you. It's possible she's kept the secret of your birth so long that to tell it now would shatter the life she's created for herself."

Jennifer was quiet for a few moments. She stared hard at Pastor Lake. "Don't you wonder sometimes what was wrong with you? I do. I wonder all the time why my parents gave me away."

"Your birth mother didn't own you, Jennifer, therefore she really couldn't give you away. All she could do was to turn you over to someone else to love and care for you. There's no point in being angry at your birth mother, even though anger is the easiest emotion to feel. I was angry for a long time myself. I wondered if I was a little toy of which they'd grown tired. I felt like a second-class citizen."

"That's exactly how I feel!" Jennifer blurted. "*Exactly*."

"Yet I feel my life might have been more difficult if my birth parents had kept me. My mother was just a youngster when she gave birth. She wasn't mature enough to handle a child. She might have hurt me or hit me or left me alone. Her love for me might have died because I was such a burden to her. She knew that might happen. She put me up for adoption so that I'd be safe and loved and cared for. It was a beautiful gift to me, Jennifer, not a cruel one."

"When you put it that way. . . ."

"I know this is very confusing for you, Jennifer, but you must remember that in most instances, adopted babies are given up out of love. They are given up so that they can have a better life than the one their birth mother could provide for them. They are placed in families who desperately want children and who have love to give. Although it might be hard for you to believe right now, Jennifer, you're not loved *less* because you're adopted. In fact, you've been *twice* loved."

"Twice loved." Jennifer rolled the words around in her mouth. "I like the sound of that. Loved twice; once by my birth mother who loved me enough to do the hardest thing she ever would do by giving me up; loved again by parents who wanted me."

Pastor Lake nodded and smiled. "When I finally came to that realization, everything began to fall into place for me. I'm not a second-class citizen because I was adopted. I'm first class all the way, and so are you."

He stood up and reached for Jennifer's hand. "Think about what I've said. Then come back and see me again. If you have any questions, call me, day or night. I'm here for you. And," he added, "your parents are, too."

As they left the church, Jennifer drew a deep sigh. "I am totally overwhelmed."

"I can see why," Lexi sympathized. "Pastor Lake gave you a lot to think about."

"Maybe I've been wrong about this all along, Lexi. I've been hard on my parents, blaming them for so many things. I really do love them. It's just that I have so many questions and so much emotion inside me that sometimes I lash out at them. It's weird, but I wish I could talk to my birth mother for a few minutes. I want to hear why she felt it was necessary to give me up. Then I could go on with my life."

As Lexi and Jennifer approached the Goldens' house, Lexi saw Peggy Madison's car parked in the driveway. Lexi knew instinctively this emotional roller coaster ride of a day was not over yet. Though Jennifer might not ever hear from her own birth mother, Lexi had a hunch that she was going to hear very soon from someone with a similar experience.

Chapter Eleven

Peggy Madison was sitting in the Goldens' living room, waiting.

"What are you doing here?" Jennifer blurted. "Was I supposed to meet you somewhere? I'm sorry, Peggy. I've had so much on my mind lately. . . ."

"Don't worry. We didn't have plans," Peggy said with a gentle smile. "I just wanted to talk to you, so I came over."

"Talk to me? About what?"

"I've been thinking about you a lot lately," Peggy admitted. "I know what a difficult time you've been having since you found out you were adopted." Peggy's eyes were wet with tears.

"That's okay, Peggy. I'm working it out. Are you crying?"

Peggy wiped at one eye with the back of her hand. "Sorry. I get emotional about this sort of thing."

"What sort of thing?" Jennifer was puzzled.

"About your adoption. I'd like to help if I could."

"There's nothing anyone can do, Peggy. This is something I have to work out for myself."

"I believe I could help you, if you'd let me."

"How could you help? How can you understand?"

Peggy glanced at Lexi, who was standing at the far side of the room.

"Sit down, Jennifer. There's something I want to tell you."

"What's gotten into you, Peggy? You're acting really weird."

"Just give me a minute, then you'll understand." Peggy patted the seat next to hers. "Please?"

"Well . . . sure." Hesitantly Jennifer sat down.

Lexi took a chair across the room, folded her hands and waited.

"I know how unhappy you've been and how mixed up you've felt since discovering you were adopted," Peggy began. "And although I can't tell you how to feel or what to do as an adopted child, I think I can give you another perspective on this situation."

"You, Peggy?"

"Me. You see, Jennifer, I gave a baby up for adoption."

A look of disbelief and confusion drifted across Jennifer's features. "Run that by me again?"

"I gave a baby up for adoption. The baby was mine and Chad's."

"Chad's?" Jennifer echoed the name. Chad had committed suicide only last year.

"Do you remember when I went to Arizona to stay with my uncle?"

"Yes."

"I had the baby there and gave it up for adoption."

Peggy turned to look at Lexi. "Only Lexi and Todd knew what was going on. They've been real friends to me. I asked them not to tell anyone and I don't believe they have. It's something I don't like to talk about or even think about, but it's important that I discuss it now. It would help me, Jennifer, if you would listen. Will you?"

"Oh, Peggy, of course I'll listen. There were rumors around school for a while after you'd left, but I didn't want to believe them. I guess no one ever knew for sure if the rumors were true or not. Chad didn't say anything and neither did Lexi or Todd. I wish I'd known. I could have been there for you."

"I probably should have told you, Jennifer. I should have let you help me, but I didn't. That's why it's so important that you listen to me and hear what I have to say now.

"Giving up your child for adoption is something that you have to do alone. I talked to my parents and my pastor and lots of counselors, but when it came right down to it, it was my decision. No one else could make it for me.

"Frankly, it's the hardest thing that I've ever done in my entire life." Tears ran down Peggy's cheeks. "I didn't realize that I could love a person I'd never met, but I loved that baby of mine, Jennifer. I watched my belly grow as the baby grew. I felt it move and kick inside of me. Sometimes I'd sit quietly and put my hand on my stomach until I felt a little fist or foot punch at me. It felt as though the baby were doing cartwheels in there. I talked to my baby every day. I told it how much I loved it and how hard this was for me. I told it that I hoped someday in its heart it would realize how much its mother loved it. It nearly killed me to give my baby up for adoption."

"Then why did you?" Jennifer asked. "Why didn't you keep it?"

Lexi knew that Jennifer was thinking of herself.

"I was just a kid," Peggy said honestly. "A kid with more than two years of high school left and no way to earn money to support the baby. What's more,

I didn't love the baby's father. I knew that I would never marry Chad. I must have instinctively known even then that Chad wasn't very stable. He was always jealous and overprotective of me. The proof of his instability came later when he committed suicide. That would have been a terrible thing for a child to face.

"I thought about keeping the baby; I really did. For several weeks I had myself convinced that I could finish high school and college and raise a child by myself. Then I started figuring out how many years it would take and how much it would cost to raise a child and go to school.

"I even called a day-care center in Arizona to ask how much it would cost to keep one baby. It was more money than I've ever earned in a year. That was only baby-sitting! I still didn't have figures for rent, food, college tuition or clothing.

"The longer I thought about it, the more I realized that for my baby to have the best that life could offer, I would have to give it up for adoption. That was the best chance that I could give it, Jennifer. I didn't give up my baby because I didn't love it. I gave it up because I did."

Peggy grabbed Jennifer's hands and held them tightly. "I don't know what was going on in your birth mother's mind, Jennifer, but I wanted you to know what was going on in mine. I gave my baby up out of love. I wanted my child to have two parents, not one. I wanted my child to have a normal life. If I'd gotten pregnant eight years later, I could have offered a child all those things. But I couldn't at sixteen. I knew that. I'm not saying that adoption is right for everyone, but in my case it was. I really believe that, Jennifer. If I didn't, I couldn't live with myself."

Jennifer was crying now, as was Peggy.

"Please don't blame your birth parents for loving you enough to do what they did," Peggy pleaded. "And don't hate your adopted parents just because they aren't your biological parents. They wanted you. They made a conscious choice to love and care for you. That's more than some birth parents do. Just because I gave birth to a baby doesn't mean that I'd have been the perfect mother. I've still got lots of growing up to do. Kids raising kids isn't such a great idea, either, you know."

Jennifer rubbed her eyes and wiped away the tears. "You don't know how much this means to me, Peggy. I've been thinking about my birth parents a lot. I've tried to imagine what they're like, and to discover a reason why they'd give me away. I'd decided that there was something the matter with me—some reason they didn't want me. Now I see that that isn't necessarily true. You really loved your baby, didn't you?"

"More than I can ever tell you," Peggy said softly.

"And you gave it away because you loved it."

"I think about my baby every day. I pray that my child has parents who are as good and as loving as your parents have been to you, Jennifer. Don't you see? Adoption is an act of *love*."

Lexi stood up to join her friends. She kneeled on the floor beside the couch and put her arms around Peggy and Jennifer. For a long moment, they hugged and wept.

Peggy was the first to break away. Her eyes were shining and she smiled. "I have to go. I promised my mom I'd be home soon." She looked at Jennifer. "I hope that what I've told you will help. Don't be so hard on your parents—any of them. They've all tried to do what's best." Without another word, Peggy left the room. Lexi heard the door close.

Lexi got up and grabbed a box of tissues from the kitchen. She handed them to Jennifer. "Here. You might need these."

Jennifer stared distractedly through the window, her eyes unfocused. "My mind is really blown, Lexi. Totally. I don't know what to think anymore. Peggy and Chad? A baby? Peggy went through all that alone. I feel so sorry for her and so sad that I couldn't help her."

"Peggy is a wonderful girl and a beautiful person," Lexi said. "Maybe you should imagine that your birth mother was a girl just like Peggy."

"Peggy is a nice girl who was in a terrible situation." Jennifer squared her shoulders. "That might not be such a hard idea to live with."

Already Lexi could see a change in Jennifer. She looked stronger, happier. Peggy had given Jennifer a beautiful gift.

Lexi jumped when the phone rang sharply beside her.

"Why don't you answer it?" Jennifer instructed. "I don't feel like talking right now."

Lexi reached for the receiver. "Hello, Golden residence. Lexi Leighton speaking."

"Lexi? It's Todd."

"Hi. What's wrong? Your voice sounds funny." As she said it, Lexi realized that Todd was crying. "Todd, where are you?"

"I'm at the hospital. Lexi, Nancy is dying."

He choked on another sob. "She's going fast, Lexi. She has pneumonia. Her kidneys have shut down. Mike won't leave her side, and Mom and Dad are trying to be with them as much as they can."

"I'll be right there," Lexi said.

"Hurry, Lexi. Hurry."

Lexi hung up the phone and turned anguished eyes to Jennifer, "I have to go to Todd. It's Nancy. She's not going to make it. Will you call Mom and tell her where I am?"

Jennifer nodded as tears streamed down her own cheeks. "Oh, Lexi. All this time I've been feeling sorry for myself. But it's Todd's family and Nancy that have really been suffering. I should be grateful instead of complaining."

Lexi grabbed Jennifer and gave her a hug. "You're always too hard on yourself."

"I don't know about that," Jennifer said. "But I do know I have the best friends ever."

She and Lexi clung to each other, feeling as though the world were tumbling in around them.

Chapter Twelve

Nancy Kelvin's funeral was a private and quiet service for her family and a few close friends.

It was difficult for Lexi to keep her eyes off Mike during the service. Though obviously saddened by Nancy's death, there was an acceptance and tranquility about Mike that Lexi had not noticed before. He was the source of strength for both the Kelvin and Winston families. After the service, Lexi got her opportunity to talk to him. "Mike?" she murmured softly.

"Hello, Lexi. I'm glad you could come."

"I'm so sorry, Mike. We all loved Nancy and we'll all miss her. None, of course, as much as you."

"Nancy was like a gift to me, Lexi. The fact that I didn't get to have her very long doesn't diminish the fact that we had some wonderful times together."

"How do you do it? You seem so calm and so strong."

Mike smiled a little. "I don't have any strength at all on my own, Lexi. Not a bit. I'm weak as a kitten. But I have a Source of strength outside myself. That's how I've been getting through the days. God is my source of strength, just as He was Nancy's. Nancy is with Him now. It may sound strange to you but because Nancy was so much at peace when she died, I feel at peace, too."

"I'm glad, Mike. I really am."

"But that doesn't mean you can stop coming to the shop," Mike reminded her gently. "My life is going to be pretty quiet and lonely now. I'm going to have to depend on Todd and his friends to come make some noise around the garage. Think you guys will be able to help me out?"

Lexi put her hand on Mike's arm. "I'll come and I'll bring Egg and Binky. They'll make as much noise as you could possibly want."

Mrs. Winston and Todd joined them. "Lexi, are you and Todd coming to the house after the service? Nancy's parents will be there."

"If you don't mind, I'd like to be with my friends for a while," Todd said. "I feel like I need a reality check—the kind that Egg and Binky can provide. It's been a long time since we laughed at our house."

"Egg, Binky, and Peggy are studying over at Jennifer's," Lexi pointed out. "That's where we'll go."

"Go ahead," Mrs. Winston encouraged. "It'll be good for you."

When they arrived at the Goldens', Mrs. Golden met them at the door. Jennifer and her friends were studying in the kitchen. Todd and Lexi were surprised to see four gloomy faces sitting around the kitchen table.

"What's wrong with you guys?" Todd asked.

Egg and Binky looked at him in surprise. "Didn't you just come from the funeral?"

"Of course I did. But that's no reason for you to

all be sitting here looking like you just lost your best friend."

"But Todd, Nancy's funeral was today."

"I know that. If Nancy were here, she'd be upset with all of you for being so gloomy."

Binky smiled a little. "She would, wouldn't she? She'd tell us to lighten up and get smiles on our faces or get out of her sight."

"And she'd give us a big lecture on how great life is," Egg added.

"My point exactly. Nancy spent a long time dying. She was ready to be with her Heavenly Father. Her biggest concern was the people she was leaving behind. So for Nancy's sake, we have to stay upbeat. That's what she would have wanted." Todd flipped through Peggy's notebook. "Now then, what are we studying?"

"If we're going to be cheerful and upbeat, we'd better not discuss that," Binky warned. "We're working on chemistry."

Lexi and Todd sat down at the table with their friends.

"Can anyone think of a topic other than chemistry?"

"I have some news." Jennifer's voice was uncharacteristically timid.

"Is it good news?" Todd wondered. "I just want to hear good news today."

"I don't know if it's good or not. I think so." A faint smile graced her lips. "I've decided not to search for my birth mother right now."

Lexi was surprised. She could see that Peggy was startled as well.

"I still might do it someday. My mom . . . my

adopted mom . . . my *real* mom . . . has said she will
help me whenever I decide to do it, but I don't feel
the need to do it like I did at first. I have great parents
who love me, who would do anything in the world for
me. I've got all the parents I need right now. Besides,
I've got all the problems I need, too, being a teenager
and all. Maybe later, when I'm ready, I'll look them
up."

"What made you decide this, Jennifer?" Binky
asked.

"Several things. Pastor Lake, my mom, Lexi,
Peggy . . . and the support group I just joined."

"A support group? For what?" Egg wondered.

"For other people who are adopted. My mom
found the name and address of the group for me.
There are kids my age as well as grown-ups at the
meetings," Jennifer explained. "It's really been neat.
I've gone twice. I can identify with everyone there
because we all have the same background—we're all
adopted. We've all been confused and had questions.
We've all struggled with the idea of being rejected or
abandoned and finally come to the conclusion that
being adopted might not be so bad after all.

"It helps to know that I'm not alone. It feels good
to have someone to talk to. And you guys have been
great." Tears filled Jennifer's eyes. "Thank you for
being so sharing and supportive. You've put up with
a lot!"

A special glance traveled between Peggy and Jennifer. Lexi knew that some of Jennifer's newfound
strength had come from Peggy.

"Besides," Jennifer added, "if Nancy could handle
her problems so gracefully, then I should certainly
be able to handle adoption almost as well. After all,
I'm not dying."

She grinned. "Why, I've just started living! Nancy taught me a lot about living life well in spite of having problems. Whenever I feel discouraged, I think of Nancy."

"That's exactly what Nancy would have loved to hear," Todd told her.

"Good. Because even though Nancy's gone, she's certainly not forgotten. She never will be. I'll have to learn to live with being adopted and to handle it. I'm going to quit thinking about what *could have been* and start concentrating on what *is*."

"Won't it still be weird, not knowing who your real parents are?" Binky wondered.

Jennifer shook her head. "I *do* know who my real parents are. They're the people I've lived with every day of my life. They're the only parents I've ever known. The only thing that they didn't do for me is give birth to me. The people in my group say that's what parenting is all about—being there for your kids whenever they need you, every day of every week, every month of every year."

"When you say it that way, it makes me think that I don't appreciate my parents enough. They put up with a lot of things from Egg and me, and they haven't complained about it very much at all." Binky pushed away from the table and stood up. "I'm going to go home for a few minutes. I have to thank my parents for everything they've done for me."

"Hey, wait!" Egg called after her. "You can't go home without me. If you're going to say 'thank you' to our folks, then I will too. Binky . . . wait up. Slow down. Binky, I don't want Mom and Dad to think I'm ungrateful. Binky. Wait up!" Egg charged out of the door, leaving the rest of the gang laughing.

Peggy closed her chemistry book. "I think Egg and Binky's parents need more than a thank-you. They deserve medals for putting up with those two."

Todd burst out laughing. "I can't tell you how good it feels to laugh. For a while I didn't think I was ever going to laugh again. Before she died, Nancy talked a lot about God's gifts. I think laughter must be one of His best."

With Egg and Binky around, Lexi mused, laughter was guaranteed. Then she looked at Todd's smiling face and realized that even in the darkest of times, if she looked long and hard enough, she would always find a light.

When Brock Taylor moves to Cedar River, he's interested in getting to know Lexi better—much better. Will their friendship ruin what Todd and Lexi share? or is their relationship strong enough to survive? Discover the answer in Cedar River Daydreams #22 to be released in September 1994.

A Note From Judy

I'm glad you're reading *Cedar River Daydreams*! I hope I've given you something to think about as well as a story to entertain you. If you feel you have any of the problems that Lexi and her friends experience, I encourage you to talk with your parents, a pastor, or a trusted adult friend. There are many people who care about you!

I love to hear from my readers, so if you'd like to receive my newsletter and a bookmark, please send a self-addressed, stamped envelope to:

> Judy Baer
> Bethany House Publishers
> 11300 Hampshire Avenue South
> Minneapolis, MN 55438

———

Be sure to watch for my new *Dear Judy . . .* books at your local bookstore. These books are full of answers to questions that you, my readers, have asked in your letters. Just about every topic is covered— from dating and romance to friendships and parents.

Dear Judy, What's It Like at Your House?
Dear Judy, Did You Ever Like a Boy
* (Who Didn't Like You?)*